In the Arms of the Enemy

Elisabeth Staab

Published by Elisabeth Staab, 2020.

In the Arms of the Enemy
Elisabeth Staab
<u>BLURB</u>:
Journal entry: 10.18.2668

I'm supposed to be leaving on the midnight transport. By the time it comes and they realize what I've done, God willing, I'll be gone. I keep asking myself why I'm doing this, but deep down I know... I know I'm doing it for her.

It's wrong to want a creature like Tatima, especially one under my guard. I can't stop seeing her dark blue eyes or feeling the softness of her skin against mine. The moisture of her lips and tongue when I assuaged her hunger.

I'm a man. I'm human. This outpost is lonely. She's as beautiful to me as she is frightening.

We trusted each other once. Maybe we could again.

Wanting her could mean so much disaster, but I can't stop.

—-

The United States has split. Supernatural creatures—lab experiments gone wrong—are being rounded up so their existence can be contained. One young man, bent on revenge, takes a job as a prison guard in order to kill the blood-sucker who murdered his father. A creature who used to be human. Someone he once thought he loved.

When Ronan gets close, he discovers the feelings he had for Tatima aren't so long-dead as he'd believed. A web of lies surrounding his father's death and the outpost where he works gets stickier the more he investigates.

The further Ronan goes, the less anything makes sense. Except the woman who can still bring him to life with a single touch.

The woman who's supposed to be his enemy.

Dedication

To the handsome lieutenant who gave us a jail tour that one time. Oh, yeah. You gave me all sorts of ideas. ;)

Chapter One

For Ronan Dempsey, living and working in North Woods Outpost rivaled dying a slow death in the fun department. Which was fine, since what he'd come here to do would most likely get him killed.

Revenge. He ate and breathed the word. He'd dream it, if he ever slept.

"Man, I've said it before and I'll say it again. I miss food. I was full-on stuffing my face with a pack of chili dogs when the rebellion hit our city. Last ones I ever had. What were you losers doing when the rebellion hit?" Ronan's friend and superior officer, Kebro, dropped beside him on a bench seat in the guard's break room. His question was mostly aimed toward the new officer across the table. A dark-skinned tank of a man by the name of Noah.

In the prison's cinderblock-walled lunchroom, Ronan folded his hands over his dry protein loaf and squinted against the flickering, brain-numbing lights overhead. Focusing on the tray in front of him, he made like he was chewing the best damn food he'd ever stuck in his mouth.

Ignore them.

This seemed to be Kebro's obsession, probing the other guards at North Woods about where they were the day of the big supernatural rebellion. Some fucked-up curiosity about what they remembered and how it affected them. Like bringing it all up again would—what?—change history? Band them all together in some sort of common brotherhood?

Perhaps after shift they'd all braid each other's hair, paint their naked chests with ancient tribal symbols, and hold hands in the ice-cold woods. Dance around and sing until their nuts fell off. Best fucking team-building in the history of never. Yeesh.

The rebellion had left the country a battered, empty shell of a republic. That it split the once United States in half, pitted brother

3

against brother, mother against son and left blood running in the streets, was enough to sicken anybody.

The horror of that entire disaster was best left in the past.

Where Ronan had been and what he remembered from the day the rebellion began sure wasn't anything he liked to discuss. Kebro knew, but he still dragged the topic out in the daylight and beat its bloody carcass.

Most days Ronan ignored the talk, because letting his nerves show would only give him away. And with every day that passed, he was one more twisted recollection from losing his own mind.

He needed to change the subject. "Hey, I heard there was a fire in the max ward right after the new prisoners came in. You guys get that handled?"

Kebro flipped his spoon. "No matter. Some strange critter they brought in who breathes flames really tried to swing for the fences when I put him in his cell."

Ronan frowned. "Is that so? I've never seen a fire breather."

"I heard the remaining ones were put down after the rebellion for being too dangerous and volatile," Noah raised and lowered his cannonball shoulders. "'A menace to human society,' I read in the *Tribute*. Never did make sense to me. You know, my sister was engaged to one of those guys who got changed from the experiments, before they started disappearing and everything. Seemed the same as when he was fully human. Treated her real nice. Wasn't his fault he sometimes lit shit up when he sneezed. I guess the rest of us don't ask questions."

The twist of Noah's lips made his sarcasm clear. "Fucked-up, if you ask me. The government created a mess, told those test subjects they could walk free, and then called back that freedom soon as some dickjockey in a suit had a panic attack about 'em being dangerous."

Kebro turned his hardened gaze toward the new guy. "They *are* dangerous, friend. If they weren't, none of us would have a job."

Kebro had specific opinions, which Ronan tried not to discuss. He'd befriended Ronan on his arrival from officer training camp. Though younger, he had rank and experience on Ronan. Like a lot of the guys, Kebro had opted for going straight to work as a detention guard rather than heading to university. Better money and no debt. After all, the value of intellectual capital was at an all-time low in this economy. Why bother?

To be fair, Kebro had a hard-edged survival instinct. Ronan had absorbed a great deal of knowledge from him. They weren't exactly the best of buddies, but contradicting him wasn't wise.

Ronan studied Noah with wide-open disbelief. He'd never heard of any human admitting to close supernatural interaction before. Not in this part of the country, and certainly not on a friendly basis.

Oh sure, most of them had had *some*. Usually though, it was unknown. Accidental. The ones who did know they'd had contact kept it real fucking quiet. It was like being exposed to a case of the pox. You didn't tell, or you'd risk quarantine.

At the least.

Ronan had been on the bus for guard training when he'd passed a group of protesting students getting led away in cuffs by the police. One of them he'd recognized as a girl he'd taken home from a bar the week before. She'd had "Howlers are people too!" painted across her bare chest and torso in black letters. A man in padded gear and a face mask had silenced her screaming with an electrified baton.

To this day, the memory seared the back of his eyes. He'd unknowingly slept with an altered creature, and God knew that could earn him a one-way ticket to getting strapped down and bad-touched at the nearest research lab. Worse by far was the sickening experience of being stuck on that bus, fists pounding the glass. The driver had only shaken his head and barreled onward while behind them Ronan's one-night stand had been beaten for nothing more than showing her true self.

She hadn't been violent, not that he'd seen. To this day, anger and guilt warred inside him. Kebro would say she'd deserved her fate. Ronan's mother, God rest her, would shake her head and ask what humanity was becoming.

Ronan wished he knew. His spoon bent in his grip.

"I heard that guy who lost the election in East America demanded a recount," Kebro said. "Fairlane, or something. No. Fairfield."

Noah waved his hand. "I heard they called it. Some people can't stand to lose, that's all."

Ronan tried to block out the surrounding chatter. There was little to be gained in unverified gossip out their way, and he never did have much use for politics. With the exception of the scant information he'd dug up about his father's death, he'd made a point of avoiding the news since his mother had passed.

The world was too fucking ugly.

Grabbing at the back of his neck, Ronan tried to rub away his lingering regret. Nothing he could have done would have saved that howler girl. Likely if he'd tried, Ronan would have landed in a cell there at North Woods instead of working as a guard. Devil only knew. Sympathizing with supernaturals had its own section now in the criminal code.

Kebro's laugh cracked in the thick silence. He pointed a spoon across the table at Noah. "Yeah. So. Your sister and that fire breather...?"

Noah turned to Kebro with a dead stare. "You have a question?"

The situation had all the makings of a disaster. Kebro might have been their superior, but Noah didn't look ready to hear jokes about his family.

Kebro was too dense or too stubborn to back down. "I mean, were you the man of the house? Where was your father? I'm surprised you people let that shit stand."

Enough. Ronan stood and dumped his full tray of food into the waste bin.

"Careful, brother." Kebro pointed his spoon and his judgment in Ronan's direction.

Dammit. Kebro could be okay sometimes. Sometimes, his rank and special privileges at North Woods as the commander's nephew made him a real splinter in the ass.

Ronan shot a glare at the man over his shoulder. "My mandatory exercise slot starts in a few minutes. Can't lift weights on a full stomach."

At that moment, his belly churned with acid. Memories played unchecked in his brain of desperate screams and falling bodies.

Kebro and Noah both nodded and resumed eating. Waste could get them into trouble. Talking shit and lazing around could also. A little chatter at meal times or in the locker rooms was about all they could risk without raising eyebrows, and Ronan's departure had effectively ended that party.

Lucky thing North Woods Outpost had a lower staff count than the other supernatural detention centers in the Eastern States. Their isolated location made escape hopeless, and few were eager to work within the outpost's walls. Ronan doubted they'd see him swing for wasting one shitty meal. Which was good, because he couldn't stay and listen any longer.

Ronan worked hard to forget about life before news of the supernatural experiments got out and the country—countries—went insane. Why bother trying to remember before when the now was all about survival?

"Hey, friend, wait one second." Kebro jogged across the small room. "Everything okay? You seem even more out in the distance than usual."

Going for a slight shrug, Ronan decided against pointing out Kebro's discussion had gone a long way toward putting him in such a harsh mood. He didn't have much in the way of friends in this place. Or anywhere. Best not to raze every bridge he'd crossed by being spiteful to this one.

"Just tired. Still getting back on track after that shift change," Ronan said.

"Aww, yeah." Kebro grinned. "Sorry." With a slap to Ronan's shoulder, his grin widened. "But thanks for switching with Neala. Needed a little stress relief, you know?"

Ronan had traded shifts with an attractive guard on daytime that Kebro had a thing for. "Sure. Nothing an orgasm or two won't cure, right?"

He scratched the achy place on his chest, taking a step away even as he threw out the joke. His purpose at North Woods Outpost wasn't to make friends *or* find solace in the arms of another.

Even still, he'd never been anyplace so desolate. Some days he thought he couldn't get any more hollow if someone cracked him open and scooped out his insides.

"Right." Kebro grinned as he, too, stepped back. "Well I'm good to return the favor anytime. You let me know."

"Actually..." Now came the real reason Ronan had willingly traded shifts with Kebro's woman. "You think you could maybe help me get a spot working on the maximum security ward? I've been looking to make a change."

Ronan worked minimum security. On the plus side, Ronan could sleepwalk through his night at his current post. In the minus column, minimum security was way the hell at the opposite end of the detention center from where he needed to be to make his plans work.

Kebro gave him a curious look.

"I've made deliveries to the wing and heard the guards talking about all the crazy shit down there. I have to see for myself."

What Ronan really needed was to see one creature in particular. No way would Kebro know. He hoped.

Kebro tipped his head to the side. "That's not a job we get many volunteers for. Believe me when I say that wing is not for pussies. Last week, I literally almost got my balls bitten off."

Ronan chuckled. "Come on. I need some action. Minimum is putting me to sleep. Soon I might do something crazy like start up arts and crafts or prayer time and shit. Teach the mongrels and parasites how to decorate their own clothes."

Ronan didn't plan on doing anything of the kind, but the joke looked like it worked on Kebro, who gave up a huge smile. "Hey, friend. Whatever you say. You really wanna check it out, I'll put in a word. I'm telling you though, that ward does things to you."

Ronan gave Kebro a friendly kick to the shin. "You takin' me for some kind of worm?"

"I said nothing of the kind. It's your fucking sanity, friend. I'll ask."

"Thanks, friend." Ronan headed for the smelly little room that passed for their gym, trying to leave behind his unease.

That ward does things to you.

He'd gotten what he wanted. Why wasn't he feeling more satisfaction?

Ronan didn't need to worry about his sanity. He figured he'd already lost his, what with his anger and pain filling up all the spaces where the rest of his feelings used to be. Anyway, he didn't plan to be around much longer. No point in trying to find peace.

Revenge. *That* was what he needed.

Revenge. Yes. The word echoed with every beat of his heart.

Chapter Two

Journal entry: 10.13.2668

I thought I'd finally be able to sleep once I got to North Woods, but I haven't. Not since I knew for sure Tatima was behind these walls. Even though the guards get far better accommodations than the critters do, it sure as fuck isn't luxury.

Fucking freezing in this place.

Anyway, I don't deserve "luxury." I figure I spent enough time dicking around when I was supposed to be studying at university, not appreciating any of the good I had. This here is my karma.

Working the midnight shift doesn't help. My internal clock is junked.

I have this constant case of the jitters. I want to—need to—get another look at her.

The parasite who murdered my dad. The woman I thought was a friend.

<u>More</u> than a friend.

Since the economy tanked and they hardly put pictures in the paper anymore, I didn't get to see Tatima until they brought her here to North Woods. Not that I don't see blood suckers here every day, but I guess I expected her to have changed more.

I expected a monster. I expected... some sign that she was different. Her dyed pink hair has faded, but her eyes are still curious and wide. She looked like the girl I remember from when she was saving up to go to college, working at my dad's company, only more beaten down. Didn't seem psychotic or savage.

Could those experiments really have turned the girl I once kissed into a killer?

I'm itching to check her name and case number, to be certain. My father was good to her. How could she have just ripped him to shreds?

I still tried to swing through the max ward at the end of my shift tonight for a look-see, but there wasn't time. Crossing my fingers that Kebro can get me in.

If I wait long enough, she might simply waste away in her cell. I hear they need blood to live, and she won't be allowed any here. I can't let this go without confronting her, though. Without finding out what she knows. What she did.

Tatima was a sweet girl when I knew her. What the fuck happened when I left??

***

Tatima pulled her knees to her chest and rubbed circles along her arms. She'd started off trying to maintain a dignified stance at all times, but curling up kept her warm. Honestly, she couldn't imagine anything she did or didn't do would change the way any of the guards looked at her.

Their eyes all narrowed when she'd walked in, some curious and some hateful. Some disgusted. Worst of all was spotting Ronan. He'd held his position behind another guard, but the wrath in that young man's stare had cut her from where he stood.

The son of Dempsey International's CEO had once been so warm. She'd even managed to entertain a crush when they'd talked at their desks and brushed past each other in the halls during Ronan's time as an intern. He'd kissed her once—barely, a gentle press of closed mouths—when she'd brought him dinner on a late night doing paperwork. His father's entrance had shocked them apart, leaving Tatima with tingling lips and flaming cheeks.

She'd find no warmth from him in this place. "I was normal, once," she whispered. Not that anyone believed her. She hardly believed herself.

The cuts on Tatima's wrists throbbed. She didn't imagine she'd be allowed to have blood or medical care, so she pressed them to her body and tried not to look, tried not to think of why she'd gotten them in the first place. Giving up on another escape attempt was something she couldn't afford, but she didn't see a way out. No doubt the *humans* would make every effort to keep her weak.

Ronan? No, he wouldn't help. The chill in his eyes had rivaled the frozen Maine North Woods outside the walls of this facility.

He looked the same as he had when she'd known him, with his olive skin, intelligent eyes, and high cheekbones. Those lips that could shape themselves into a generous smile when they wanted. This time, his furious expression told her that he believed he knew her story, and like the rest of the Eastern States, he'd already had her tried and convicted.

Tatima looked around her cell for the thousandth time. Aside from a blanket for sleeping, a drinking fountain, and a metal receptacle she used to relieve herself, she had nothing. Nothing, except metal and stone.

This is it, Tati. You have to think of something, or this is where you're going to die.

Chapter Three

Ronan managed to drift off and woke shortly before lunch to the sounds of the guy in the room next to his praying for death. Since the dorms were laid out in small shoe-box rectangles with back-to-back bathrooms adjoining the bunk areas, he could hear every scintillating one of the man's heaves and groans. He tried to mentally drown it out with the noises from outside—movement on the grounds and far off echoes in the halls—while he stepped into the narrow shower stall and gave himself a quick shave. Whatever the man had, Ronan hoped to the fractured fucking moon and back it wasn't contagious.

The previous winter, some viral thing had swept through the compound. The lack of staff left an opening for massive violence to overtake the minimum security ward. The supernaturals didn't get sick the way humans did, and the guards had all been vulnerable.

The incident had happened before Ronan's arrival. Learning of it made him nervous, but it hadn't changed his plans. Soon as he'd stopped drinking and throwing shit at the walls after his father's death, he'd hit the nearest recruiting center for para-guard training.

Seemed like the higher-ups had learned to take precautions against illness, mostly. Now they were all given vitamin injections to boost their immunity. Not that Ronan relished getting those shots.

Ronan blasted his teeth with the UV sanitizer, licking his dry lips as he laid the little cleaning wand on a small shelf over his sink. The only other personal item in the tiny bathroom cubicle was a small cup for water, which he never used due to the shortage. Drinking from an uncertain water dispenser could leave a guy manning one of the outpost's stainless steel thrones like it was his new guard station.

He eyed the moaning, groaning wall. "No offense, buddy, but I don't wanna end up sounding like you."

He pulled on his clothes, sitting on his cot to dress because his head came uncomfortably close to the ceiling in his sparse room. A hand through his short hair to tame it, and then he hurried to the door. Today was soy butter sandwich day. He didn't completely hate those, and his stomach growled for a change.

At the door he spotted the reminder scrawled on his calendar. Fuck. Kebro had told him that if he wanted to get moved to the max ward, he needed to present an updated physical. So much for sandwich day. Still, he'd deal with hunger for the physical that would get him closer to Tatima. The max ward was the shit job nobody wanted, and since the creatures had no freedom to move outside their cells, staff count was at its lowest.

He'd be able to move freely. Exactly what he needed.

Most of that day he'd lain awake, wondering how things had gone down. Wondering if it was completely delusional to want to question her. Would she be honest with him? The court documents had been sealed, so Ronan only knew what scraps of information he'd been able to read in a weeks-old Eastern States *Tribute*. The names, the places, the fact that Gerard Dempsey, age sixty-two, had been mauled to death by a parasite named Tatima Sloane.

"Tatima." Ronan's mouth twisted on the bitter taste of her name. He'd always liked her name. It would be pretty if she hadn't done something so ugly.

She would be pretty if she hadn't turned into something inhuman. If she hadn't committed an act so brutal.

So...animal.

Ronan traced his fingertip around the box on the calendar, picturing her in the short glimpse he'd gotten when the duty guards walked her into North Woods on the evening of her arrival. He'd met her wide stare for a moment that lasted forever. Remembering her indecipherable gaze made his blood rush with things he couldn't understand.

Ronan took a breath and examined the painted stone ceiling. The *Tribute* column hadn't given specifics, but after the uprising, some supernaturals in the Eastern States had been allowed to remain free, provided they were being monitored for medical study by companies like Dempsey International.

Ronan had left home well before the massacres, so he didn't know quite how his father's company was involved, but Dempsey International had doctors and research scientists on staff and had brought many pharmaceuticals to market. Ronan could only assume Tatima had gotten involved in some study his father had taken up after Ronan's departure.

Ronan would never forgive himself for the fact that he had no longer been at home when his father was attacked. He'd disappeared to escape the pain of his mother's death. Gone off to be a screw-up.

He tapped at the calendar, as if it had answers. "Gotta talk to her." He'd done so much wrong. For once in his life, he *needed* to do this the right way.

All the way out there in what the government referred to as the "Dead Zone," little communication flowed. He'd never know the details of his father's death any other way.

She might refuse to talk. She might lie.

She might. He was probably, as the kids liked to say, hitting the Cryptanaphine pipe too hard. Still, he'd never know anything if he didn't try.

Not knowing, not having been there when his father died, left a hole.

Then again, he'd been present when his mother died, and that had been a fucking nightmare. Ronan shook his head and left his room, turning down the hall toward the rear exit of the building. Maybe there was no answer.

Death. Nothing uglier.

***

Tatima bit into her tongue. Needles of sunlight jabbed into her skin. Outside her face remained placid. Inside, she screamed. Long and loud, she screamed.

She tried to distract herself as the guards marched her and a chain of prisoners across the dirty expanse from the medical place back to the jail. It helped to focus on how she'd gotten beaten with the backwards end of the lucky stick. The extra gene they'd planted inside of her could have mutated her into any number of species—a howler, an elemental—she could've been one of the ones whose body rejected the experiment and died an unrecognizable mess of fur and bloody, broken parts.

She'd seen the failures. Oh God, had she seen them.

So she told herself that after having been duped into those medical trials, the result could have been far worse. Having wound up in a cinderblock coffin far away from the only thing in her life that mattered? The argument didn't work so well.

She'd woken one day with a thirst for blood that couldn't be filled. She suspected then that her life was over. She wished it had been.

Now she was here. Now they called her a parasite. *Parasite.* As if she were one of those hideous worms that burrowed into people and used their bodies to lay eggs.

They made me what I am, and then had me crucified.

Staying angry kept her going in the moments when she wanted to give in. She couldn't afford to let go. Not if there was a way to find Valo.

All the super-human strength or powerful hearing in the world wouldn't matter one bit if she withered in this place.

A shadow crossed Tatima's body. She opened her sagging lids to see Ronan scowling, thick arms crossed over his chest. "What's going on? Where are you taking these guys?" He turned toward the guard who led their haggard bunch of prisoners.

If Tatima hadn't known better, she'd have thought Ronan had a howler inside. The way his question boomed low and deep, and his nostrils flared with displeasure. The way his broad chest swelled with purpose.

Judging by his uniform, Ronan didn't appear to hold command at this outpost yet he held himself with a broad-shouldered dignity all the same. His serious countenance fit him far better than his father's had. Gerard Dempsey had been kind, but muddled and hands-off in his old age. This man...this man always had wheels turning in his head.

The question was, would this bring more trouble for her?

The beefy guard ahead of Tatima jabbed the prisoner at the front of the line. "Took 'em to medical for vaccinations. We're taking them back to their cells."

Clouds darkened across Ronan's stormy face. Tatima couldn't read his expression clearly with the glare of day shining behind him. She'd always been taller than the average female, but he topped out over six feet, and lifting her eyes directly toward the enlarged sun would blind her for a week.

"Why now? Why during daylight?" Ronan's demanding tone boomed in Tatima's ears.

Dammit, she used to love the warmth of the sun. She'd put herself through part of college by waitressing at a tiny cafe, where she'd sit at an outside table once her shift had finished and read novels endlessly instead of studying. She'd bring the pages close to her face and smell their gentle mustiness while she dreamt of other lives and places.

She'd been doing that very thing when a man from Dempsey International approached her with a business card asking if she needed to make some money. She *had* needed money.

Her economics textbook had been sitting on the table in front of her that day. All students needed money. Surely, the man from Mr. Dempsey's company had known. He'd taken an easy opportunity, which Tatima had so stupidly fallen for. She'd worked for Mr. Dempsey that summer and he'd been such a nice man. She'd thought she could trust his people.

Her misstep meant she'd never sit outside a coffee shop smelling old books again. She wouldn't even if she could.

The guard leading Tatima's little group shuffled and matched Ronan's defensive posture, seeming reluctant to answer his question. Perhaps because he didn't appear to hold any rank. His words, however, came out again in a quiet command that nearly gave Tatima the urge to answer on everyone's behalf. "They needed vitamin boosters," the guard finally said.

Vitamins. Tatima rubbed her cheek against the aching spot they'd punctured on her upper arm. She hated to think what they'd put into her. Surely it couldn't have been something to benefit her health.

Ronan stared at her. He seemed to hesitate. Then, with a swift but light touch, he ran his hand across the back of her arm. "This one's burning. Get them inside."

Tatima swallowed a surprised breath. The brush of his skin on hers sucked her back to that brief kiss in his father's offices years ago.

She could still smell the gentle spice of his cologne. Feel his skin brush hers. His smiling eyes on her face stirred fluttery warmth in her belly that day.

Today Ronan looked entirely different, but so familiar. The complete detachment on his face almost convinced her that the heart-stopping moment they'd shared had all been in her head.

Funny how only a few years could be a lifetime.

The guard pointed his electric baton at Ronan. "Whatever. This isn't your detail, friend. Not your say."

"What, you wanna have to haul her back over to medical again?" Ronan's head whipped around. "Fuck are you thinking, taking parasites out when the sun is high?"

"We had orders." The guard from the back this time. A stout, hairy man who looked at Tatima as if she were a dessert and he hadn't eaten sweets in ages. She'd seen that look too many times. It filled her with the urge to bare her fangs and claws, but that only made everything worse. She knew from experience.

"Whatever. Get 'em inside." Ronan studied Tatima again and stomped away, heading in the direction they'd all come from.

Once, she'd scheduled a last-minute lunch for Ronan and his father, and he'd left a thank-you note on her desk. "Thanks for being amazing," it had said. With a smiley face. Certainly Ronan didn't think her amazing now.

No. He thought she was a monster.

Yet she had to wonder as he glanced over his retreating shoulder, if he hadn't been trying in some way to help her. Was that too much to hope?

Probably.

Certainly.

When the line surged ahead and paused inside the blessed dimness of the building, Tatima indulged in a moment to rest her face against the cool concrete. Stopping earned her a baton to the ribs to get moving again, but she didn't care. Much.

If her eyes stung with pain and humiliation, she didn't notice. Really didn't.

It would be a comfort to think Ronan had been trying to help her back there in that courtyard. Under the circumstances, the comfort came with a high cost.

If she got past the cool touch of his skin, she could see logic. His father had told her that Ronan had been sweet as a child, but driven past his limits by unwittingly helping to develop the drug that killed his own mother.

Given the look on Ronan's face when he'd drawn close, the way he vibrated with conflict, perhaps in spite of hating her, he simply wanted to do right.

The idea lifted her head.

The circumstances of their reunion were unfortunate. If she looked beyond his furious eyes and the snarl that crooked his lip, she could see her cloudy memory hadn't done him justice.

He was far too handsome a young man to wear such an ugly expression.

Tatima hoped some kernel of the old Ronan was still inside that angry guard. Too bad it wouldn't be enough hope to save her life.

Chapter Four

Journal entry: 10.15.2668

I was thinking today about the first journal my mom gave me. I thought it was stupid and stuck it on a shelf. Then Rekennah Willows broke my heart, and I sat down to bitch about how she'd shredded me. A decade later, I still write about the things I can't say out loud.

Running into that chain gang yesterday—running into Tatima—left me fucking confused. I didn't expect to see her up close yet. Touch her. Feel her skin burning under my hand in the midday sun. I swear, inside it made me boil so bad I wanted to kick the ass of every idiot in that place. And then my own, for feeling protective of the one creature I'm supposed to hate.

Hate.

Not rub her arm and read the fucking riot act to her guards.

But I remember meeting this shy girl who had pink hair and shiny silver hoops in her ears. Whose cheek dimpled when she smiled. Friendly, but shy.

I can believe in the justice of taking a life. I didn't sleep through every class in school—if a person commits a crime, they are likely to commit that crime again, or escalate to worse—then again, what's worse than murder?

If Tatima killed my father, taking her from this world would be removing a menace and it would also give me absolution for failing my parents.

Even if Tatima is guilty, I've never believed in torture. What I saw today was torture. I couldn't let it stand.

That guy next door still sounds ill. He hasn't been out of his room. I'm wondering if I ought to start wearing my sick mask. I haven't needed it in all the time I've been on duty, but since we're the only outpost for an eternity, getting anything that goes after your immune system is death.

Maybe everything is death.

I think about that a lot. Death. I signed up for this outpost when I first heard they had a suspect in my father's murder, the nearest supernatural detention center to where it happened. Chances were good the killer would be brought here.

She was.

Humans convicted of murder no longer get to choose how they die. In a society once overflowing with technology, they've done away with the incineration chamber and the laser-fire squad. Now, it's back to one very sharp blade, and one man you better fucking pray has the backbone to remove your head from your body with a clean whack.

I wanted that privilege with my father's killer. To take my revenge with a blade.

Now that I've seen her face again, so many questions are threatening the sharp edge of my rage.

***

They weren't supposed to wear any kind of ear protection unless it was for shooting practice. But holy fuck, Kebro hadn't been kidding about the screams. Prior to getting reassigned, Ronan had only caught brief snatches before of the sounds that emanated from the max ward.

He had one word: *primal.*

He kept stride in the disturbingly puke-colored hall while Kebro showed him what was what on the ward. He didn't have time to pause and wonder what the fuck had caused the creature in cell 8-A to shriek, but the sounds echoed in his chest. Curiosity sure as hell had its scabby little claws around his throat.

Sounds like that came from torment. Suffering. Thing was, the creatures bunked solo and couldn't have anything in their cells. Food at meal time came served on a bio tray. Crumbled to dust if you tried to break one over someone's head. A small blanket. Their clothing and undergarments.

Nothing more. Nothing to hurt them, and nothing with which they could hurt themselves.

Ronan realized he'd allowed his curiosity to wander too far from Kebro's rundown. When his pal asked if Ronan was clear on everything he'd said so far, all that that came up in Ronan's head was static. That, and the lingering howling sounds, long after the real noises had died away.

"Absolutely." Before Ronan could think, he'd snapped out the lie.

"Good." Kebro's skull twitched under his buzz cut. His curious gaze sharpened under a flickering hall light. No further questions came, but he looked as if he might be reserving judgment.

Anyone wanted to judge, they'd need to line up behind Ronan himself.

"Moving on then." Kebro punched his palm. "Here's what's most important down here in the beast's belly." They passed door after nondescript metal door with nothing but a Glassite window and a food slot as they headed down the long corridor. Finally, they came to a stop at a utility closet with an electronic lock and a scanner pad.

"Lay your palm on there, friend. Make sure you've been keyed in correctly."

Ronan's palm met Glassite, followed by the sounds of buzzing and clicking. A small light over the touch pad changed red to green. Kebro nodded, and Ronan pulled the door wide open. "What's in here?" They had a similar closet in the minimum-security ward, mostly for emergency access to the outpost's gas lines, and for storing a handful of cleaning supplies. The layout of this one was a little more crowded, with shelves of boxes.

Kebro waited for them to get inside the room to answer. Motion sensors made lights come on, an eerie reddish glow that made the walls look bloody. "All righty, friend, prepare to have your mind blown. This shit in here..." Kebro's eyebrows bounced with apparent jubilation, "...is how us pure humans ensure we maintain our spot at the top of the food chain." His fingers walked over to the boxes, and the rows of vials inside. "You noticed the insulated doors at the entrance to the ward, right?"

"Sure." Ronan's muscles bunched at the base of his neck. "Why?"

"This entire wing is kept separate from the main building. Power, air flow, and water supply." He turned to the other wall and made a circular motion with his hand, indicating three panels. He twisted the large screws at the top of one and lowered it to reveal an opening. Under the strange crimson lighting, his grin turned sinister. "Water supply."

Ronan nodded his understanding, even though something Kebro wasn't saying hovered just out of his mental grasp. "I see." He wanted to ask what the hell his buddy was getting at, but he waited. Something fluttered in his chest, and not in the I'm-about-to-get-an-exciting-surprise kind of way. "So what is all of this?"

Kebro popped a tube from one of the shelves and stuck it into the hole for the water supply. With a swift sucking sound, the contents disappeared. "That, my friend, is the most hard-core cocktail of supernatural ass-kicking shit known to human science."

Chills danced a creepy tiptoe across Ronan's back. "Some sort of... sedative?" No, it was something far more. Ronan couldn't say for sure what told him, although the smile on his superior's face sure as fuck served as a clue.

Ronan fought an inner blackness nudging at the edge of his brain. Whatever this was, he didn't want to know. He didn't want to be involved.

Leave. Say you've changed your mind.

"Oh, sure." Kebro's grin broadened. "Sedatives. Blood thinners for those parasite vamp motherfuckers. Shifter suppressant for the mongrels and whatnot." Kebro cracked his neck. "The real kicker, is this drug called Ellanol, which is—"

"I know about Ellanol." Ronan's gut roiled. He seethed, nerves crackling enough for him not to care that he'd interrupted Kebro's explanation. Tensions ran high in these detention stations, and rudeness could start dustups. He swore silently and sucked in a breath, fighting back his sudden nausea. "My father ran the company that produced Ellanol. I interned the summer it was formulated, but we scrapped it when testing went badly." *When it killed my mother.* "The stuff did more harm than good. It was branded as a volatile substance. I thought it was removed from the market."

Kebro raised his eyebrows. "Sure, for humans. It's been repurposed."

"How come I didn't hear about this before?" Ronan tightened his joined fingers behind his back. He tried to take a calming breath and couldn't. He shouldn't care, but he couldn't stop the flood of icy horror pumping into his chest. Was this honestly something his father would have approved? "You're poisoning them."

"You're new to this ward." Kebro tapped his temple with one finger. "You didn't need to know." He flipped the panel shut for the water supply and tapped on the nearest shelf of vials. "Once at the start of your shift, once at the end. Typically the whole mix keeps 'em weak enough, tired enough, so they're easy to manage. If there's a scuffle when you're moving 'em to the showers or whatthefuckever, you can throw in another at the midpoint, but try not to exceed three in one night. The evening shift gives 'em one dose too. Ellanol has some nasty side-effects, and we've got too much on our hands to tangle with cleanup. Clear?"

Ronan nodded. "Like a starry sky." Still interlaced behind his back, his fingers tingled and went numb. Ellanol had been named after his mom, a drug formulated to combat the rare blood disease raging through her system. Horrifically, it had not only killed the disease, it had killed her immune system and gone on to eat away at her body from the inside out.

Ronan knew exactly what that stuff did, because it had done it all to his mother. He tried to get this new information to make sense in his head as the memory of his mother's death burned behind his eyes.

They were giving this shit to the supernaturals, who supposedly were tougher than humans to kill. They wouldn't be with Ellanol pumped into their bodies.

That was probably the point.

Kebro hadn't come out and said so, but the implication circled in the air around Ronan's head. He told himself again that this made it easier to pull off his revenge plans, but instead horrible things rose up in his throat. Nausea. Protests. Poisoning a bunch of clueless inmates had "fucked-up" painted across it in giant letters.

Ronan stared at Kebro, suspecting he ought to heel-toe it out of there before something came out of his mouth that would land him in as much trouble as all these North Woods inmates.

He scrounged in his mind for some way to cover. Some clever response. All he could see was his mother on the floor.

Kebro's arm snaked around Ronan's shoulder. "Hey now. Wipe that conscience off your face. You think those fuckers wouldn't turn on you if they had the chance?"

"I'm sure you're right." Ronan fought against the twitch of his lip that threatened to inch up into a sneer. The brush of Kebro's hand wiped sweat onto Ronan's face. Something that never would have bothered him before suddenly made him want to wipe his face on his buddy's shirt. Then plant a boot in the center of his chest. God, what the hell was this?

"Goddamn right," Kebro said. He nodded like he was pleased to have Ronan's agreement. "This stuff ensures the population turnover stays high so we don't have overcrowding, and it keeps them compliant so we don't get our asses kicked. Now, some of the ones out in the regular population, their labs or owners might eventually reclaim them or they might get really lucky and earn their freedom." Kebro snorted like he'd told a joke.

"But listen, you have to know that here in the pit, there's no escape. They've been brought here to max because they're *evil,* Ronan. They've committed violent crimes. Signed away their chance at freedom. Only thing we're doing here is giving them an express ticket."

Kebro punched open the door to the small room with both fists. "Now. Regional supervisor's coming for monthly inspection during the day today. To keep it looking like we uphold certain protocols, they all have to be taken to shower. Each one should be provided with a blanket if they don't have one. Same procedure as usual, and maintain your vigilance about the cuffs."

"Roger." Ronan parted ways with Kebro, who headed off down the bend in the long arm of the max ward. *Whistling.* Was there another one of these access panels that dumped into the water supply over there? Probably.

Another wave of queasy agitation slithered through him as he led the creatures, one by one, back and forth to the shower. Disquiet slithered through his brain, churning in his stomach as he pondered this new information he'd been handed. He'd been blissfully ignorant of this detail and probably so much more in the months he'd spent working down in the minimum security branch, waiting to come face-to-face with the parasite who murdered his father.

For Tatima. Who would be in that cell, drinking the poisoned water.

Like Kebro said, if they were guilty they deserved to die. They'd landed here for crimes, after all. For killing humans.

If they were guilty. According to the *Tribute,* Tatima hadn't even had a trial. After the massacres, judges had been given the power to pass summary sentencing on paranormals. And to die the way his mother had...

Ronan coughed, trying to inhale the stale air in the ward. He passed cells with screams, cells with grunts and moans... one with a sweet song seeping from the cracks around the food slot.

He paused, even though he shouldn't. Looking inside the cells carried risks. But it was her. Through the small rectangle of a window, he caught a glimpse of her now-faded pink hair, and then the rest of her. Long legs tucked to her chest, clad in a mauve jumpsuit.

Huddled in a corner, she'd wrapped her still-burned arms around herself. She shivered, looking cold. When he'd seen her in the courtyard before, she'd held her head high in spite of the apparent strain she felt from the sun's rays. Now, she looked even smaller, the way she was all curled-up. She rocked there, singing a song once sung to him by his mother about monkeys swinging in the trees. He caught sight of a small water fountain across from her, and thought again about those vials.

He'd been there when his mother had passed away. Whatever these creatures had done, poisoning them to death would be painful and cruel.

It was the coward's way to kill.

She must have felt his stare, because she got quiet and lifted her head. For longer than Ronan would ever admit, he found himself trapped by her stare. Again. Her eyes, dark blue and shaped like almonds, reflected an undefined vulnerability that made everything else in Ronan's mind go silent.

Ronan hadn't been in this place long, but long enough to see evil. He'd seen the blank-eyed looks on sociopaths; the hard, threatening stares of angry guards, and even the sneaky I've-gotten-away-with-something glimmers in the inmates' eyes. Her eyes showed him a lot—fear, anger, and the same recognition he'd gotten when he saw her outside the courtyard.

No murderous rage. No challenge. Not in the courtyard, and not now.

He clenched his fists. Was there a chance he could be wrong about her?

A hint of vulnerability appeared when she glanced away, sinking her front teeth into her lip. "Is there something I can do for you, Ronan?"

Chapter Five

Ronan turned his back on Tatima's cell and trekked down the hall. He entertained the notion of starting the showers with her to save face once he'd been caught staring, but he needed a minute to get his brain facing the same direction as the rest of him.

Heaviness filled his stomach while he walked each detainee to and from the showers. Each time, Ronan swallowed a sharp sensation jabbing his throat.

The things he'd learned tonight churned up his emotions. Confusion tumbled around with the other thoughts in his head, mixing up everything. *Everything was wrong.*

He'd signed on for guard duty at North Woods so he could confront his father's murderer. He'd shown up for training full of rage and guilt and righteous indignation, certain that he would make the bastard pay.

Once he knew it was Tatima, betrayal and shock had joined the mix of emotions, but his rage had burned steadily. And yet... once he'd seen her again up close, his thirst for revenge met a thousand other emotions.

Memories—good ones—stubbornly poked through the fog of Ronan's fury. The taste of Tatima's lips. The warmth of her laugh. Her hand on his. The conversations they'd had together in the sun on their lunch break, and how much he'd enjoyed them. Add to that what he'd found out about the Ellanol and his insides tied themselves in knots.

If he did absolutely nothing, Tatima would be dealt a far worse death than Ronan could have ever planned. If the doubt that nagged his insides held even a drop of meaning, then that would make everything worse.

Ronan reexamined Kebro's logic—fucking *basic human logic*—tried to think about the fact that some of these guys really were monsters. Not simply because of their creature status. After all, if they'd never done a thing except smile and help old ladies cross mud puddles, they'd be hanging out in the minimum-security ward. Perhaps they wouldn't be in North Woods at all. Nevertheless, Ronan couldn't shake the idea that this situation happening here was wrong.

He tried forgetting that he'd heard her singing in her cell. Saw her clinging to herself like she was freezing and frightened. He hated that her song lingered in his mind. Her voice had actually sounded... pleasant. Melodic.

He hated that her hair had dulled and the smile he remembered had disappeared entirely. He wasn't sure he could afford the sympathy. He wasn't sure he could afford not to sympathize.

When he couldn't avoid it any more, he rubbed his achy stomach through his uniform shirt and went to take Tatima to her shower. He'd saved her for last, hoping it would give him more time to think. More time to spend with her. Hoping it would give him the right words.

Everything jumbled together in his head. At first the only word he had was "arms" when he asked her to put her wrists out so he could cuff them. Once he had her in the cuffs, in front of him in the hall, paranoia kept his eyes bouncing everywhere in the long corridor. Kept his lips sealed tightly for fear of what might be heard.

In the brighter lights of the shower area, with its groaning plumbing to mask their conversation, he chanced another look at her face before unlocking the cuffs and letting her in.

He studied her features, fine-boned and practically regal. He hadn't noticed that before. Her skin still carried a blush it shouldn't have.

Never touch the prisoners.

Cardinal rule. Well, he'd already broken the rule once—albeit with witnesses and in a show of making a point—and lightning hadn't fried him where he stood. So much desperation had shown on her face out in that sunshine. Try as he might, that suffering was something Ronan couldn't ignore.

Ronan swept a finger along her cheek. He wasn't sure what the skin on her cheek ought to feel like if it were healthy, but he checked anyway. "The burn seems to have faded. Is it painful?"

She frowned. "It's better."

"Good." He swallowed. Licked his lips. All the moisture in his body had evaporated into nowhere. "You should let me know if you think it needs medical attention."

She flinched. "And who's going to care?"

Ronan jerked his hand behind his back. "Just let me know if it gets worse."

Maybe she wondered why he cared at all. Him. Of all people. *I wonder myself.*

Maybe he needed to prove he still had some decency left.

After escorting her to the shower, he watched her more carefully than he should have. It was so wrong, but he couldn't seem to tear his gaze away. Call it morbid curiosity. Was she the same as the howler he'd been with, the same as she'd been before, with a body like a normal woman? They'd been told so many things about these creatures in training.

Based on his limited observation, at least some of those things he'd heard were lies. He saw no scales, no tail, no sharp protuberances along her spine. As far as he could see from his view through the shackle portals in the shower, she really did look like any human woman on the outside. Her breasts looked full and high, not shriveled or discolored. Perhaps her ribs showed more than they should, but her body still looked curvy and perfect in all the right places. She hadn't changed much at all on the outside.

The man in him found it hard not to react. The guard in him, the dutiful son in him, the human in him, felt so wrong about such base intrigue he wanted to clock himself in the jaw.

Then Ronan saw the scars. She lifted her long hair to rinse it off, revealing puckered scars that dotted her upper back. Cuts marred her wrists. Her arms. Maybe a suicide attempt after her capture. The ones on her back, though, she couldn't have done herself.

I wonder what happened to cause those scars. I wonder why I care.

Tatima started humming again. Quietly, and probably with the assumption that Ronan couldn't hear or see her. She took a handful of soap granules from a dispenser, lathering between her fingers as she turned to face his direction.

"Shit." Ronan spun away, but not before he noticed her turn her face up to the spray.

Had she gotten any in her mouth? Was the water supply for the showers the same as the drinking water?

One by one, he mentally rifled through every file he'd read, every *Tribute* column that listed one Tatima Sloane, twenty-four years old, as his father's murderer.

Just because she seemed nice before and she comes in pretty packaging doesn't mean she isn't capable of murder.

So why was he sweating under his uniform at the thought of killing her now? Because it wasn't simply killing her. It was *poisoning her...*

The drug was named after his mother. She never would have wanted to be the namesake of something this vile. He still couldn't make the sweet teenage intern he'd swapped jokes and little notes with match with the monster he'd read about in the *Tribute*. In fact, each time he saw her, it got harder.

It all made sense the day he walked into North Woods. None of it made sense now. He wished he had his parents to talk to.

Fucked-up part, of course, is if he still had them to turn to, he wouldn't be in this place.

***

He's staring.

Tatima's senses had been enhanced considerably when she went through "the change." Every twitch of Ronan's fingers around her arm, every pulse of his breath in her ear, spoke volumes.

Conflict and recognition blazed bright and clear in his deep eyes. He might be a guard, but he was a man, too. She'd caught him sneaking a look at her in the shower. He liked what he saw. He hadn't wanted to, but he did.

Perhaps there was a chance of convincing him to help, after all.

They paused outside of her cell so that he could unlock the heavy door. "It was nice of you," she whispered. "To be concerned for me."

"I don't want you keeling over on my watch is all." His eyes darkened. He set his shoulders and clamped his jaw like he meant to make a point.

"Of course." She leaned closer. Not too close. Not enough to be threatening or make it seem like she might try to bite. Only enough to brush her shoulder against his. "Still, it was appreciated. You were always kind."

A nervous flutter twirled in Tatima's center. Such a statement could stir up a dormant nest of flesh-eating wasps, but she hoped thanking him for being a good person would spur Ronan to act accordingly.

Should she press for further discussion or wait for another time? Perhaps she could get him to relax around her more. The decision was made for her when a door opened at the opposite end of the hall, and boots approached at a steady clip.

Tatima took one step away from Ronan.

Ronan took one step away from her.

With one hand on the metal door, Ronan pressed the other between her shoulder blades, pushing her into the room with a jerk of his chin. They stared each other down while he unlocked her cuffs through the slot in her cell door, but nothing more was said.

By the time he was done, he looked angrier than before.

Chapter Six

At the start of his next shift, Ronan realized he'd conveniently forgotten to put the Ellanol cocktail in the water. Hadn't even gone back to that command center at the end of the hall. He froze in his tracks as he made the initial loop around his half of the ward, wondering about the implications.

Honest mistake. He'd been busy. Overwhelmed by the monkey wrench in his plans, more to the point. By his strange encounter with Tatima. Should he get questioned, he'd say that first part.

Missing one time probably wouldn't do much. Course the whole not wanting to send people to a slow, torturous death thing...that would be a problem over the long term. Ronan gritted his teeth and cursed himself for the inconvenient burst of conscience that had sprung up right in the bull's-eye of his vengeful rage.

Those doubts sent a spider web of cracks through the steel inside his heart and soul. Every time he let himself dwell on them, the once-sure foundation on which he stood at this outpost shifted beneath his feet.

He turned to the side, aware that he'd stopped right next to *her* cell. For reasons he couldn't name, he stood there and read the placard next to her door, even though it was all information he'd burned into his brain: female, blood-sucker, age twenty-four, Tatima.

Murder.

How could she have killed his father? She'd known him. Worked for him.

Ronan closed his eyes, once again picturing the questioning look he'd seen in her eyes. The fear and hope.

"Is everything okay?"

He didn't flinch at the sound of her voice through the door, but it was a near. He'd heard the parasites had extra-good hearing, but Ronan figured she was asleep in there since she made no noise on the other side.

To save face, he dropped his knee to the painted, concrete floor. "Sure. Fine. Tying my boots." Once again, this act put Ronan on the naughty list. One of the very basic rules of this place was to never put your face near the food or cuff slots. It was supposed to open only from the guards' side, but creatures had found ways to take advantage in the past. For all he knew, he was seconds away from her skewering his eyeball with a piece of metal she'd snagged from a door handle. Even her fingernail.

He couldn't explain even to himself what he was doing. He kept his ears alert, as much for movement in the hall as for the possibility of her next words. They hadn't spoken much, and he didn't like the way the dark satin of her words slid right into his brain.

Except that he *did* like it.

"You know, I remember seeing pictures of your mother in your father's office. I never said so, but you look so much like her."

Ronan's shoelace dug into his hand.

Shifting noises just on the other side of the door. Pressure, a tiny clink against the metal of the meal slot. She didn't try to open it, but from the sounds of things, she moved closer to lean against the door. She made little tsk-ing noises, like he should have known better. She was right, he *should* have known better.

"No response, Ronan? You used to be chatty. I guess we all change when we get older. Your father certainly did."

His fingers twitched. "About my father. I need to know... I need to know what happened." His breath rushed out, his chest tightened. No way she'd tell him, but he wouldn't get anything if he didn't ask. He'd been trained to use force in interrogation, but he didn't want to.

Not on her.

Another shift on her side of the door. A loud breath, another clink of metal. "I'll tell you anything you want. I don't have any secrets."

Journal entry: 10.17.2668

Tatima didn't tell me a thing. Before she had a chance, Kebro showed up to tell me he took care of the water the night before since I forgot last night. Fucking great. Turns out they track who scans into the room.

The next time, I scanned my hand, but then I didn't make the drop. Wonder what my prize will be when they catch on to that trick? I kept a vial in case they count.

I wish Tatima didn't have such a sweet-sounding voice. Hearing it again, I can remember talking to her over the phone back when I interned for my dad. It makes me question things, confuses me. I should remember that sirens have pretty voices too, and I heard a gang of them led the charge in one of the bloodiest and most lethal battles of the rebellion. Made city blocks' worth of human heads explode. Can't go by pretty or sweet.

I can't trust my own judgment right now, but fuck me, I can't do the thing with the water.

It's poison.

***

Ronan got himself excused from the pre-shift check-in by saying he had to take a piss. He caught the guy finishing the evening shift heading for the control room—Armin, his name was—and gave a friendly wave. "Hey, everything all quiet tonight?"

Armin scratched his head. "Actually, yeah. Evening shift can be weird sometimes. Most of these beasts are nocturnal, and most of them are waking up mid-shift. Usually damn pissed-off." He shook his head. "Guess I would be too, stuck in a cell out here. Sucks enough being one of the supposed people in charge," he mumbled.

Ronan nodded. "Hey, listen, you done the pour yet?" *Have you dumped the poison in everybody's drinking water yet? Jesus.*

"Heading there now."

"I'll take care of it for you. Do mine later on."

Armin cast Ronan a smile of gratitude. "Great. Thanks, friend. Dying to get off my feet. These boots, you know."

Ronan knew. His feet hurt already, and the midnight shift hadn't started. He watched another guard leave, not sure if he should agree with Armin's assessment of outpost guard suckitude. It wasn't a cushy life, but they weren't stuck in cells being fed toxic chemicals.

This was, after all, the situation they'd all chosen. The one Ronan had chosen for himself. To serve humanity and repay his father for not being a better son. To garner his revenge.

Oh yeah, that plan that was now so royally screwed. That one.

He chatted with Armin about more inane nothingness at the mouth of the ward, and then killed time while he pretended to inspect the seals on the doors through the rest of shift change. Guards passed in the halls on their way elsewhere, and Ronan wanted to be sure the activity had died down before he got to his plans.

"Hey, Ronan. Everything good?" Big Noah walked by, a rifle slung over one shoulder, on his way out to cover the perimeter. He gave a slight wave. Since the day Noah and Kebro had nearly faced off in the break room, he and Ronan had run into each other off and on. The big guy mostly kept to himself, but had always seemed decent enough. He edged over in the hall now, bringing himself closer.

Ronan tried to pretend he wasn't hurrying back into the mouth of the max ward to avoid conversation. "Sure. Starting my shift." He motioned toward the sealed doors, ready to head down the hall. He liked Noah better than most of the guards in the place, but tonight wasn't a night he wanted to spend time making friends.

"Me too." Noah nodded as if he agreed with Ronan's plan to heel-toe it off to their shifts, but slowed down anyway. "So how is it on the max ward? Heard crazy stories."

"It's..." He'd meant to throw out something meaningless and easy. *It's fine. Great. A laugh a minute. Best job ever.* The look on the big man's face gave Ronan pause. So did his memory of the other man's disapproval about the way humans treated supernaturals. If he could trust anyone with his doubts about this place, perhaps it was Noah.

"It's what, huh?"

"It's fine. Actually, it's not that bad." Too many ears in the halls at shift change to take the risk. Ronan grabbed for the door.

"Good to hear, friend. Sounds like it wouldn't be any picnic, some of the shit these places pull." Noah tapped his arm before turning to go. "Me, I don't know if I'd have the stomach. You have my respect."

Ronan frowned at Noah's statement, which sounded strangely loaded. "Hey, Noah."

Noah stopped mid-stride. "My friend?"

"What do you mean? What kind of shit?" Ronan hadn't known until he'd gotten to his first shift on the ward. How would Noah?

"You don't have to ask me. You already know exactly what happens on max, my friend." He came closer, lips hovering right next to Ronan's face. "I think your real question might be whether it's worth the price." Noah pulled away and shot Ronan another look over his shoulder before he disappeared.

Mind spinning, Ronan wiped a hand over his face and went down the ward to the control room. He scanned in, took one vial from the shelf, and slid it into the cargo pocket on his fatigues. Upon exit, he unhooked a pair of cuffs and stopped in front of Tatima's door. "Arms," he said quietly.

The time had come to get answers.

Chapter Seven

When Ronan brought out the shackles, Tatima complied without a word.

There was little option to do otherwise. Surrounded by more stone and steel than she could beat her way through, fighting now would only weaken her when she needed to stay strong. Better that she work harder at getting on his good side. Finding a way to warm Ronan's icy barrier might be her best chance at escape. Maybe her only chance.

When he opened the door, she kept her face still. A cyclone of fear spun inside her when Ronan radioed to another guard somewhere that he was taking a prisoner to the medical facility.

Medical. Why?

Breathe. Tatima shivered, sucking frozen, antiseptic air into her uncooperative lungs as Ronan directed her down the hall. She wanted to ask questions but couldn't open her mouth to speak. She made her mind blank inside, nothing but a ball of static and blackness. Nothing of the horror that had led to her becoming who and what she was now.

Medical facilities meant pain. Tests, and torture. The touching. Medical facilities were the worst prisons of all. They had turned her into a blood-thirsty creature.

Not that Ronan would understand. If he did, would he care?

As they passed down the hall and through the outer security doors, a sniper in a tower kept a laser trained on them the entire time. On her. The tiny dot of light bounced against her as she walked.

She glanced to the dot on her chest, then up at the sky. She did her best to ignore it, instead looking up at the cloudless indigo night painted with glittery white light. With a deep breath she said, "It feels like it's been forever since I've seen the stars."

At her comment, Ronan's anger seemed to re-crystallize. "My father will never see them again."

Wrong move, Tati.

Right then, tears she'd spent forever trying to hold inside threatened to break free. Ronan had been so sweet to her once. She didn't want this man to hate her.

Her eyes squeezed closed and stayed that way as they walked. She let Ronan guide her over the scrubby, pitted ground at their feet, not sure she cared whether he let her fall. She batted around the possibilities. Should she apologize for something she hadn't done? Stay quiet? Profess her innocence?

He wouldn't believe her if she did.

"I liked your father," she said at last. "He always seemed like a decent man." Unfortunately, he'd been too far removed from the goings-on in his own company. At least he had been, until the night he got killed. Then again, Ronan had gone even farther away.

Even standing in the frigid nighttime, Tatima's insides burned at the memory of that night. She'd been held—helpless—caught in a place worse than Hell. Now everyone she loved was gone. They'd thanked her with this horror.

"Then why did you kill him?" His harsh whisper sliced through her heart.

She lifted her chin and met the fire in his eyes. "I didn't. You have to know I couldn't. But—" How could she hope to make him understand?

She took a long, deep breath before she continued. "Can you... try to imagine..." Another gasp of the frigid air. Heaven knew when the sting of fresh night air might fill her lungs again. "I was a starving student, Ronan, even after working first to put money aside for my family. I was approached by someone looking for test subjects. Someone from your dad's company, so I believed them to be reputable. It sounded easy. I needed money, so I signed up. How bad could it be, right? It sounded like easy money to help pay for school." She took another long, deep breath before she continued. Squeezing her eyes shut against ugly memories allowed moisture to slip out past her closed lids.

No, it hadn't been easy. At first it had only been painful. At first.

"A few tests led to more. They needed blood. Tissue samples. Hair. There were... injections. Some of the time I was put to sleep. I'm not sure what they did, but I don't believe it was to measure my resting brain patterns as they claimed."

Ronan's fingers tightened on her arm, digging into her flesh. "That doesn't sound like anything my father would have sanctioned."

She glanced around, shivering in the night air. "I think a lot of effort was put into keeping it hidden. And even *we* didn't understand what was being done."

He stopped walking, his brown eyes shimmering under what was left of the moonlight. "If you didn't know what they were doing, why let them lay a hand on you at all?"

"Imagine what you would do in my place. At some point in the process, someone comes to you, says that what you gave wasn't enough. That they need more blood. To do more tests. Maybe even harvest more organs. If you comply, then they say they'll offer more money. If you refuse, you leave with nothing. I'd signed a contract. I couldn't afford to walk away."

More tears gathered around the rims of her eyes. "Eventually I *did* try to leave. I said no, and then I was told I was no longer classified as a human due to my altered genetic structure. So I could either stay in that testing facility or come to one of these detention places. What was I supposed to do then?"

"We need to keep moving," Ronan growled and grabbed her arm, marching them both forward. "Is this some kind of lie, or do you have a goddamn explanation for what happened to my father?"

He doesn't believe me.

Everything inside her threatened to explode outward at once. She couldn't cry. Not now, not with this man, of all people. She could hope he would be of use to her, but she could *not* make the mistake of using him for comfort. Hurt and frustration threatened to crush her. "They tricked us. Or maybe I didn't ask enough questions."

"Your father, I don't think he was running things anymore. He stopped by for visits now and then, and the penalties were harsh for anybody who spoke out while he was on site. So he didn't know what was happening. The day he found out was the day he got killed. A man named Fairfield is who all the doctors and staff seemed to report to."

Ronan shook his head. "Fairfield?" He looked confused. Confused, but thoughtful. He'd slowed his steps. "I remember a Fairfield, but he was some mid-level manager last I knew. What did he have to do with running the lab experiments?"

Tatima tried to stop the memories of Fairfield's hand on hers. His smoke-scented breath in her ear. "Plenty," she whispered. "He did plenty."

"What did he do?" Ronan stopped with a scuff of boots in the dirt. His fingers gripping her elbow softened, squeezing.

She wanted to tell him. She simply couldn't. "Why are you taking me to the medical facility, Ronan?"

He cleared his throat. "I needed a way to get you alone so we could talk. I'll tell them you've got a stomach ache or something."

The excuse sounded reasonable enough. It didn't relieve the anxious hollow in her middle. "But why?"

From the side, he had a strong, proud nose. His jaw muscle twitched and flexed as they once again headed toward the medical facility. "I told you, I wanted to talk."

"You think I killed your father. I know you do. It's why I've been brought here." She swallowed. The frigid night seeped into her, penetrating her skin, making her numb. "If you're planning on doing something to me, I'd appreciate if you got it over with."

Ronan spun toward her. "I wanted answers. I wanted to know why you killed him. I thought I knew who you were once upon a time, and you *said* he was a decent man. So why?"

Tatima's chest ached. "I told you. I *didn't*. I swear. I would never have hurt your father." Her fingers curled in frustration. "We only tried to escape."

Covered in the shadowy overhang of the medical building, the darkness enshrouded them both. The laser sight from the guard tower didn't seem to reach to their tiny corner, but she hardly dared to relax. Maybe this would be where he tried to kill her.

Was there any chance she could pick up enough speed to outrun the guards and scale the fence? She could get out of the cuffs easily enough. There was still the razor wire, but at least they'd gotten out of the building.

"I read the reports. A human couldn't have—"

"It *was* one like me," she scoffed. "Parasites, you like to call us?" Hideous word. Made them sound like ticks. That was probably how the humans saw them. Disgusting and easy to smother.

She thrust her shoulders back. "Think about it, Ronan. You knew me before. I didn't have fangs when I worked as your father's assistant. I was fully human until someone from your father's company came and talked me into signing up for what I thought were benign pharmaceutical tests. I was only turned four years ago."

Ronan paused like he'd had a revelation, but then he shook his head. "The conversion experiments were supposed to have been banned by then."

That thought always made her feel like she was choking. She'd always hated to watch the news. Depressing stuff. Now she wished she'd been better informed, that she'd understood they were doing something illegal.

"It's an interesting phrase, 'supposed to.'"

Ronan gripped her arm. "You mean—"

Noise across the compound told them they would soon have company. They locked stares, both understanding that they couldn't be caught simply chatting in the shadows.

"You need to hurt me," she said. "They won't believe a story about stomach pain. Nobody cares if one of us has a simple tummy ache."

Tatima pulled her shackles from behind her back. Ronan stared at her like she'd lost her mind.

"Yeah," she said. "Easy locks on those things. Too bad they aren't my only problem." Grabbing a knife from Ronan's belt, Tatima stuck the blade into her side before she could think better of the plan.

"The fuck—? Are you crazy?"

"They're coming. There's no time." Tatima doubled over, choking on the fiery pain that spread through her side.

"There... that should make them believe." She handed the knife back, hilt first. Then she handed over his cuffs. "You'll need to put these on me again."

"Shit." He snapped the cuffs onto her wrists. "You've been able to get out of those all along? What are you still doing here?"

Tatima sighed. She'd played a hand she shouldn't have. "Like I said, those aren't my only problem. Believe me, I've tried."

As Ronan pulled close to secure her hands behind her back, his guarded expression slipped, leaving behind etched lines and something hard to define that lodged itself under her ribcage.

"The scars."

"A reward for my previous attempts."

"You can't simply wait for an opening and run?"

Why is he asking this?

She shook her head. "Shackles are easy. Many armed guards, snipers, a wall, razor wire, and a thousand-mile journey to safety? Trickier. And every day, I'm weaker."

"You're all convicted criminals. Of course they're going to keep you weak." Ronan's fingers tightened around hers. He probably didn't even realize.

Frustration pushed her nose to his. "How many are truly guilty," she whispered. The fear, the pain she'd seen on her fellow prisoners' faces, the intensity and the horror of it all made her throat burn. "You acknowledged yourself, those experiments were supposed to stop but they kept going. I wouldn't be here at all if they had. The second we were no longer useful, Fairfield tried to have us destroyed. Your father's death was a tragic accident, but the young woman who killed him was only trying to stay alive. You would have tried, too. Anybody would have."

Tatima shook when Ronan grabbed her by the arms, staring hard into her face. His lips parted, a desperate breath escaping like he didn't know how to respond. His gaze roamed around, searching her face in the near dark. Looking for what? Truth?

Ronan's palms burned Tatima through her clothing. He took a step, and then another.

Her stomach tightened.

Footsteps came closer.

"I have to get you inside." He shook his head and looked her up and down. "You're bleeding."

"I know." Had he forgotten? She hadn't.

"Get ready." He leaned down, breathing a bare whisper into her ear. "When I hand you off to the duty officer I'm going to have to make like I'm roughing you up a little." He tugged her cuffs, presumably to make his point. He pulled her back to his front, pretending to get her under control. "You're sure it was Fairfield who was in charge?"

"I'm sure." God, it almost sounded like he might believe her. She was afraid to hope.

Ronan's lips brushed her ear. "Listen to me. Don't drink the water on your ward,"

"What?"

"It's poisoned. Don't."

Her pulse jumped. Why was he telling her this? Maybe she'd misheard, or the blood loss had fogged her brain. Was he honestly helping her?

He spun, leaving Tatima in the hands of the clinic guard, with confusion and panic clogging her throat.

God, if Ronan might be on her side, she had a chance. If he wasn't....

Then it was only a matter of time.

Chapter Eight

Ronan tapped the table in the satellite room and adjusted his timepiece for the billionth time. While he waited for the data to load, he flattened his fingers, drummed a beat that lacked rhythm, adjusted his uniform, and did the whole thing again. All while reminding himself to act natural before somebody came in there and asked him what the fuck he was doing.

He got the slick marketing page for his father's company to load, but then the connection crapped out again. Still, it was enough.

Dempsey International, Inc. Helmsman: David Fairfield.

Fairfield. He'd known a manager named Fairfield. A lot must have changed for him to climb to the pinnacle of Dempsey International. Kebro had mentioned a candidate in the Eastern States election named Fairfield. Surely a coincidence. Suddenly Ronan wished he followed the news.

Dempsey International's short-form company history had his father stepping back to focus on family and charity work after the death of his wife.

Except his father's only family would have been Ronan, and he'd gone off to school to escape the pain of losing his mom. Hell.

He closed his eyes and forced himself to sit with the burn of regret while it slid down his center like a razorblade. He'd left because his father's life had been enmeshed with the company, and once Ronan disappeared, his father had stepped down.

Tatima had been right. And Ronan hadn't known.

I should have stayed. I should have done so many things differently.

Had Fairfield weaseled his way into power after Ronan's father decided to retire? This information might not be irrefutable proof, but it lent credibility to what Tatima had told him.

Ronan pushed away from the table. For the first time since stepping into North Woods, he felt like he could breathe. Maybe there was no need to kill. At least, not her.

He had no idea where Tatima actually was at the moment. She hadn't been brought back to the max ward the night before. Rumor was there had been a dustup over at the clinic and she'd been thrown into solitary. He didn't know how to reach her. Nobody he knew had access.

Maybe if he went to the commander, he could fake his way through finding out more information. The higher-ups had access to things the grunts didn't. He checked his watch. He ought to be heading to bed, but he could come up with a reasonable lie.

He'd only been in the commander's office once before at North Woods, to debrief on a fight he'd broken up between two howlers in the minimum security yard. Territorial, those guys. Ronan's night had ended with getting a rabies shot and washing piss off his favorite pair of boots.

He knocked quietly but firmly on the door frame and waited for Commander Keller to look up. "Mr. Dempsey. Enter."

Tall, bald, and unassuming behind his steel desk, Keller was probably about the age Ronan's father would be. Sometimes Ronan looked at the guy and wondered how a man like him survived the supernatural rebellion when so many others had been killed. The commander didn't look like much on the surface. He didn't fill out the uniform with an imposing presence the way a huge guy like Noah did—the way some even said Ronan did.

Once in a while though, Keller got a certain sharpness in his gaze. Obscurity lurked under the surface of Commander Keller's "nothing special" demeanor. That curious ripple under the surface was so easy to forget, and Ronan might if he hadn't seen a blip when he was standing there.

Still. Better safe than royally fucked. Ronan made an abrupt change in course. "Thank you, sir. Sorry to drop by unannounced." Shit, if he didn't trust the commander enough to ask for info, why was he here?

"My door is always open. I've been meaning to speak with you, anyway."

Uh-oh. Ronan's neck itched. "Sir?" Perhaps he didn't need a reason to be there.

Keller shut the file he'd been reading. "Close the door, will you?"

Ronan did as asked, and a rushing pulse joined the suspicious tingle in his scalp.

"It's come to my attention that one of the creatures you're guarding is known to you personally. Is that correct?"

Well, the man wouldn't ask if he didn't already know. "Yes, sir." Ronan kept his breath steady, and prayed his nerves didn't show from across the room. "I assure you, sir, it's not a problem."

I swear it hasn't made me question my world view or my loyalty to this job or what I believe about my humanity in general. At all. Really. Except for the fact that by "not at all" I mean totally and completely.

The commander regarded Ronan from over the top of his glasses. "Can't have it, young man." He huffed through his nose. "Now, I've looked at your files, you seem like a good kid. Spotless record."

A memory of brushing his lips against Tatima's ear slapped Ronan in the face. For the slightest second, his fingers had slipped through the slippery strands of her pink hair. He wanted to feel those strands of hair between his fingers again.

"Thank you, sir." His mind took a quick trip to the vials of Ellanol sitting in an old boot box under his bed and he swallowed. Yep. Spotless fucking record. At least, until he got caught.

The commander nodded. "Nevertheless, it's a conflict of interest. I can't take the risk of you going off half-cocked and taking matters into your own hands."

"Of course." Funny that they were pulling him so he couldn't do the thing he'd already decided he probably shouldn't do anyway. Ronan's pulse tripped as he opened his mouth to ask the question he knew would take him from flying under the radar to a blaring red blip front and center on the screen.

Still, he had to know. "Sir, aren't they all going to die anyway?"

The commander removed his glasses and placed them on the desk in front of him with a half-smile. "Those prisoners are part of a study, son. Terminating one of them early throws off the sample group."

Well, fuck. *Fuck.* This wasn't just about keeping prisoners compliant. This was another experiment. Ronan held his breath, because he was afraid of what he'd do or say if he opened his mouth. Something about the commander's smile looked wrong. Cold, measured, and assessing in a way that made Ronan want to clench his fists. So he only nodded a slow, deep head bob, like, "Oh, right. Sure. That makes perfect sense." When he thought he could control his face, he said, "Understood, sir." Meanwhile, his stomach tried to disappear inside of itself.

The commander made a note in a file. "I'm going to have you transferred back to minimum security." He grinned, back to acting warm and grandfatherly. Sure, cuz he was concerned about the well-being of his dying detainees, after all. "Low stress. You're looking a little washed-out there, son. You look like you could use some rest."

Minimum security. The other end of the fucking compound from where Tatima was supposed to be. Ronan needed to find her.

He went with the first plan of action that popped into his head. "Actually, sir. I *have* felt unwell. The guy next door to me has been ill. I may have caught his virus. I came here to ask about leave. I have a few days built up. I could use the rest, and I wanted to see about traveling home to pay proper respects to my father and mother."

The commander cast his eyes to the stone ceiling while he appeared to consider. "I don't see why not." He flipped open a folder. "Looks here like you've got four days. Tell you what. I'll give you through the weekend. Make sure you don't pass whatever you have to anybody else around this place. Report back for your new shift on Monday."

Ronan blinked. "That's generous. Thank you, sir."

Sweat chilled on the back of his neck as he left the commander's office. He hoped he'd thrown off the commander's suspicions, but he needed to move fast.

"Hey, friend." Noah-the-Tank stood waiting outside in the hall, along with a slightly smaller man. "Done talking with the commander? We're waiting to speak with him." Noah cracked his knuckles and flexed his fingers as he spoke.

Ronan gestured with a casual wave. "All yours." He paid little attention to Noah as he walked away, thoughts chugging. His neck cracked when he turned to look down the stark cinderblock hall, doing nothing to ease the throbbing tension in his muscles.

Things kept getting more screwed up. What little he'd managed to find out about his father's company led him to even more questions. He needed more information from Tatima.

First, he needed to find a way to get to her. Fucking fast, because they didn't have much time.

***

Good damn thing they kept it so cold in the North Woods Outpost, because the ridiculous lie Ronan was about to tell had him sweating.

What was happening to him? He'd been the kid who followed rules to the letter in grade school. Who tattled on the other kids for stepping out of line. Until his mom died and he ran off to college, anyway, too drunk to give a shit what anyone else did.

Hello, comfort zone? I don't think we can see each other anymore. It's not you. It's me.

He approached the guard outside of solitary confinement, a guy he vaguely knew from training. Ronan made his face as hard and nasty as he could manage. "Hey, friend. Finn, right?"

Finn looked perplexed. Probably didn't get a lot of action down here in the solitary cells. "What can I do for you, comrade?"

Ronan lowered his voice. "Listen, I need you to do me a huge favor. Gotta see the parasite. Tag number A-5. Got a grievance to settle."

Now this was where Ronan had to act like the biggest parasite-phobe in the Eastern States and hope he was talking to one of the many humans who'd had a problem with a creature somewhere along the line. He'd be fucked if this guy turned out to be one of the ones whose mother had been best friends with an energy-leach who helped deliver her first baby or some crazy thing.

Finn looked around, unsure. "I'm... not allowed to..."

Okay. Finn was a rule-follower. Ronan could respect that, he just needed to find Finn's bargaining leverage. "Listen, she did a real number on Doc Naier over in the med unit. Guy saved my ass once. Us grunts, we gotta stick together, right? What would you do in my position?"

Ronan's harsh, impassioned whisper almost pulled up a gag. The levels of fucked-up here were too many to count. A month ago, maybe even a week ago, Ronan might have said these words and meant them. Sure as hell, he wouldn't have been using them to sneak quality time with a woman who was supposed to be his enemy.

Finn squeezed and wrung the back of his neck. Again, he looked around. "You can't— If you hurt her I could—"

Ronan threw out the same grin he used to use to get girls into bed. Not that he was trying to do that with Finn—handsome SOB though he was—but it was the same concept. Show sincerity, show warmth, then get the fuck gone before she figured out you didn't plan to call back. "Just wanna convey a message, if you know what I mean. No visible marks. I swear."

Now, hey. That last part was true. He was here to find out what had happened to Tatima. He didn't intend to hurt her. Ronan fought the urge to physically look behind him to find the place on his well-planned path where his goals had changed.

Finn checked his watch. "Okay. I'm, uh, I could use a break anyway. Gonna go take a leak. Grab some amphetamine crystals. Make it speedy. Hope you know what the fuck you're doing." Before he walked away, he slapped his hand on the red panel that would unlock Tatima's cell.

Ronan slid inside. When the door shut behind him and his eyes adjusted to the dark cell, he lost his mind.

"Tatima, holy shit. What did they do?"

They'd taken her clothes. Curled in a corner, with her hair draped around her knees to provide her only cover, Tatima shivered violently. She bled visibly, too. In the near dark of the room he couldn't say for sure, but it came from either the hands clasped to her knees, or from her legs. The smooth beauty of her skin now appeared dingy all over, covered in some mixture of dirt and blood.

His stomach twisted at the sight.

Ronan bent to the floor and put his arms around her. Whatever had happened between the night before and now, she'd been hurt even worse. He needed to help her. He couldn't ignore his gut on this one, or it would make *him* the monster.

"Tatima, what happened?" He pulled his jacket off and slipped it around her shoulders.

She shook her head. Her only answer was to bury her head between her knees.

Ronan laid a hand on her shoulder. "I'm here to help, okay? I need you to help me in return. You were trying to convince me you didn't kill my father. Next thing I know, you're down here for violent behavior. Please talk to me."

Her responding laugh was so bitter and dry that Ronan's own tongue tasted the acid. "You know, I've learned the hard way some people are... fascinated by those of us who have been altered. It's a kink, I guess. The doctor—"

Ronan drew a sharp breath. "Jesus." He gripped her arms. Acid shot into his throat. "I'll kill him. I left you there—I'm so fucking sorry." His hands traversed her skin carefully, trying to touch her with respect, trying to assess if she was hurt... meanwhile, war waged inside his skull.

"No." She pushed her forehead against his. "*No, Ronan.* He didn't... He thought I was sedated enough, so he tried to take me out the back door so nobody would know." A thin sob escaped, rattling Ronan's insides. "I stopped him. I held a syringe against his throat," Tatima whispered. "I knew it was a gamble but I had to try and get out if I could. I had to."

"Thank God." He hugged her tighter. She'd attacked, but she'd done so in self-defense. He hated himself for having put her in the position to need to do such a thing.

She wiped a hand across her eyes. "That's why they sent me here."

Breath rushed out of Ronan's lungs. "I'm sorry. I'm so fucking sorry." He pressed, one cheek against hers, trying to apologize with more than only his words.

Christ, whatever that asshole had tried, nobody deserved that. Ronan wrapped his hands tighter around her shoulders, mindful of her wounds. Mindful of the fact that Tatima wore no clothing at all.

It's my fault for taking her to the clinic. Ronan wanted to move his hands, to make some sort of comforting gesture, but didn't want to wind up harming her instead.

Her swallow sounded like a struggle. "Your father. I swear I didn't kill him." Still pressing her face to his, hot breath fanned against his cheek. "I swear. Freyenne, she was a friend of mine. She was also Fairfield's pet."

Pet…as in he'd *owned* her? "That's—I don't understand. I didn't know him well, but I remember him being vocal against par—" He cleared his throat. "Against supernaturals. Do you have any…?" He let the question die. If she had proof, she wouldn't be here.

She shook her head against his. Still, she wouldn't open her eyes to look at him. "If I had any proof, don't you think I'd have shouted it from the top of your father's building?"

"Yeah, it was a stupid question. I just… There has to be something. Do you remember hearing or seeing—"

"I've got nothing. *Nothing, Ronan.*" The hopelessness in her saturated every word.

"I hear you. I'm sorry." It didn't even feel strange when he pulled her close, tucking her head into the crook of his neck for comfort.

She jerked, letting out an agitated growl. "Ronan, no. You have to go." She shivered harder now. Her fingers dug into his arms even as she told him to leave.

Carefully, he put his hands to either side of her face. "What's wrong? Why should I leave?"

What was he doing? He'd gone from wanting to slice her throat to wanting to provide comfort, but he couldn't bring himself to believe in anything but her when he touched her skin and smelled her hair. He remembered every minute they'd shared, every look and every touch, and he couldn't believe she was lying.

Vaguely, he wondered if this was some sort of mind game. He'd read about that shit in the books at training. But he remembered the look of desperation on her face. Perhaps it made him stupid, but he believed her story. Moreover, thanks to him she'd been preyed upon by the clinic doctor. He owed her something for that.

"Ronan, think." A husky, inhuman noise rumbled from her throat. "You're in a cell with an injured parasite. I heard you send the guard away." Her lips parted, and Ronan's stomach fluttered at a pair of extended fangs shining through the dark in front of his eyes.

"You're saying..."

"Ronan, I'm thirsty."

Chapter Nine

Even though she'd come to expect it, the hunger hit her hard.

Tatima tightened her hands into fists and bit down on her tongue. All at once desperate to strike, she held herself rigid and waited for Ronan to back away. She had a warm, fresh, alive human right in front of her. Touching her. His blood rushed hard and fast, pulsing in waves under her hands. She could feel the pulsing of his heart with her heightened senses.

She wanted to move, but couldn't. If she tried to back away first, her resolve might snap.

Ronan's hand slid across her cheek. His fingers threaded into her hair, curling and finding purchase, making themselves at home.

Tatima imagined that maybe the gesture was meant to comfort or apologize, but it also brought Ronan's wrist right in front of her lips. Right there, hardly an inch from her mouth, with its juicy veins.

Oh, God. Ronan was young. Healthy. He smelled vital and masculine and his blood would contain so much power. The guards here, they were given good food, she bet. Vitamins. She'd be strong again.

Her lips parted. Her gums and fangs ached, seeking a target. Inside, Tatima's blood beat swiftly with anticipation. With fear. Ronan had come in here acting as if he meant to help her, after all, and here she was seeking to bite him. Who knew what he'd do?

Ronan rose onto his knees. "Wait." Fabric rustled as he pulled his jacket tighter around her shoulders. "It's not much," he said. "But you need to keep warm. Now. You're right, I'm gonna have to go soon. I'll be back, though. I have a plan. What can I do for you right now?"

She shook her head. "Really. Please. You have to go." She needed his help. His trust. If she bit him, he wouldn't trust her anymore.

"Hey, listen." He grasped her chin. "I didn't come here to hurt you. Do I believe you about my father?" He dropped his hand, shrugging against her arm in the dark. "I think so. I'm not sure. I'm willing, at least, to look for more. Right now we need to help each other. So tell me what I can do."

"I told you," she whispered. "I'm thirsty." As Tatima uttered the words, another growl rose in her stomach, drowning out her thoughts. She grasped the hand Ronan had held in front of her lips only a minute before, drawing a deep breath, taking in the tangy scent. "You have lovely veins." She didn't want to take from him without permission, but running her thumb over the plump conduits under his skin, his flesh so close to her mouth, made her head light.

"You need this to survive?"

Tatima nodded, hovering with her parted lips barely brushing his skin. "It's what the experiments caused. I'm stronger, but I have to feed this constant hunger."

Ronan let out a low moan above her. "If I have something you need, then you should take it."

She scraped his wrist with her fang, not quite breaking the skin. "Ronan, when I came to this place, you looked at me with murder in your eyes. Now you're offering to save me?"

"Tatima..." His breath came in jagged puffs. "You're naked, cold, and starving. I'm doing the best I can with a wretched situation. If you aren't responsible for my father's death, I want to find the person who is. You need the blood or your wounds won't heal, am I right? Eventually, you'll die?"

"Yes."

"Will it hurt me? Kill me?"

Tatima gasped and dropped Ronan's hand. "I would never hurt you."

"Then take what you need."

So she did. Warmth seeped into her as Ronan drew close, drawing her hair away from her body and pressing against her. The ache inside abated, the numbness and the chill chased away with each swallow of Ronan's gift.

When Tatima repositioned her mouth, sliding her tongue across Ronan's wrist and ensuring she had a tight seal with her lips, Ronan drew a surprised breath next to her ear. His fingers trembled against her. She smiled to herself, enjoying, if only for a moment, this small shift of power.

For the past few years, Tatima had been at the mercy of men who'd tried to control her. Tricked her into being used. Taken advantage of her. Hurt her.

Right now, even though Tatima was the one imprisoned, she read his quiet gasps and groans as fascination and surprise. He held himself so still, as if transfixed by her drinking from him. The way he flexed and released his fingers told her that he resisted an inner urge to grip tighter. He wouldn't hurt her.

Tatima sighed against the spicy sweetness of Ronan's skin. The way he held her, had her wishing they had known each other far better when they'd both worked at his father's company. Perhaps if they'd kept in touch after Ronan went away to school. Perhaps if she hadn't rushed off like an embarrassed child after being caught kissing...

So many roads not taken.

She didn't know why he was helping her now, but she was grateful. Maybe they could help each other.

With his free hand, Ronan moved a stray lock of hair from her shoulder. Fingertips brushed her collarbone, then further down where she'd gotten the tattoo symbolizing Valo's footprints in that brief time when she'd been able to go free.

Ronan's finger stopped, but the ink did not sit flush with her skin. He had to have discovered the mark. He tapped lightly. "I... I shouldn't have, and I'm sorry, but I glanced at you when you got in the shower before. It's stupid, but we'd been told all these things about how supernaturals were disfigured. I guess I fell for too many lies. "

The peaceful haze that had settled in with Ronan's blood fled as panic rushed in to take its place. She pulled away, sealing the bite.

"You have a mark here. What is it?"

Tatima gripped Ronan's hand, willing him to understand. Telling him this truth could make him want to help her. It could also make him turn away. "I have a son." Her throat burned. "I tried to get myself out of the testing program and leave. When I found out I was expecting, I got it so I'd always have him close to my heart."

Tatima's senses picked up the rapid flapping of Ronan's heart. "Where is he? Where is his father?"

"Valo is being held in the lab, I hope." She swallowed. "His father? I don't know. He was a lab technician, and he was fired. I'm not proud of it, but when I found out what was really happening in the study I seduced him to get him to put me in the control group. The control group didn't get the altered DNA. They stayed human, and eventually got sent home." Her eyes burned, and shame washed down her face. "It didn't work. More tricks, more lies."

Everybody lied.

Ronan wrapped his fingers around hers. "I'm sorry."

"Stop." She pulled her arm away. Immediately, she wished she hadn't. "I'm sorry. You're trying to help. You haven't—"

"Yes I have." His head swiveled around. "Fuck, I don't want to leave you here."

She shook her head. "You have to."

He looked around again, as if another option might appear. What could he do, walk her out the front door? Naked?

"Ronan, it's okay. Just go."

He did. He left.

It hurt to watch him go, even knowing he had no other choice.

***

Journal entry: 10.18.2668

I'm supposed to be leaving on the midnight transport. By the time it comes and they realize what I've done, God willing I'll be gone. I keep asking myself why I'm doing this, but deep down I know...

What she told me about that mark... her son.

I keep seeing those tiny feet. I have nobody. Who's going to look out for Tatima's child?

Not a bunch of lab guys. I know what they'll do.

Something's wrong around here. The dark cloud hanging over North Woods Outpost has to do with more than the weather.

My father's company, my mom and me—those were his loves. When mom died, he wasn't the same, but I pulled away, too.

I regret that I ran. I want to make up for letting him down. I thought I could do that by taking revenge on his killer, but now I don't believe Tatima's guilty. Even if she is, I'm not sure murdering her would settle the score.

There's a child who doesn't deserve to pay for others' sins.

My father's dead. She has answers. I want them. I'm no longer convinced she deserves the end this place is sending her to, which makes me wonder how many of the rest of them are actually guilty of crimes.

It's supposed to be wrong to want a creature like her, especially one under my guard. I can't stop seeing her dark blue eyes or feeling the softness of her skin against mine when she touched me. The moisture of her lips and tongue when I assuaged her hunger...

I'm a man. I'm human. This outpost is lonely. She's as beautiful to me as she is frightening.

We trusted each other once. Maybe we could again.

Wanting her could mean so much disaster... but I can't stop.

She's as beautiful as I remember. Maybe more. Maybe it's something deeper. Like the way her skin warms against mine, even in the freezing cold. Or the way she had the balls to plunge a knife into her own stomach and march into that med unit. Maybe it's because even knowing who we are to each other, she still seems to be placing her faith in me.

I'm not sure I've ever seen anybody so fucking brave—except maybe my mom when she knew she was dying.

If it were me in a cell in this place? I think I'd have gone out of my skull already.

I've asked myself if I can trust Tatima in return, but I think deep down I've made my decision. Must have, given what I'm about to do.

I hope I'm right. I swear though, the look in her eyes, the feel of her in my arms. If I'm wrong about this, I'm the biggest idiot on the planet and I deserve what I get.

Part of me worries that she trusts me because she has no other choice, and that makes me awfully... aware. I don't want her to turn to me because I'm her only option.

I want to be worth her trust. I haven't felt worthy of anything in a long while.

I wasn't the best kid I could have been, especially to my parents. It's uncomfortable to hear her say my dad told her I was a good kid. I didn't work too hard in school, even though my mom always pushed me to study. I was smart so I got away with slacking off. I thought I could atone by putting away the supernaturals who threatened to overtake humanity.

But are they as awful as I'd been trained to believe? Tatima's got no scales on her body. No signs of mutations that I saw, and I saw pretty much all of her. What other false information have I been given?

That howler I took home with me right before guard training was sweet and wild in bed with a mouth that would give an outpost guard a run for his money. I had enough fun with that girl that I bought her breakfast at the diner near my apartment and kept her number for maybe another date sometime. Except then I left to come here.

What if Noah's right? Tatima? Humans created supernaturals. I read it was originally supposed to be some military experiment. Bio-enhanced soldiers or whatever.

Except it didn't work out, and now we're trying to put all the subjects down. If it's true, it's fucked.

Maybe she's faking it, but Tatima hasn't shown a single ounce of murderous rage. Hard edges, sure. After being in this place a few months, I've got hard edges, too. Everyone does.

Things are all messed up.

I have to help her. I have to.

***

In spite of the plain, windowless doors, Noah's room in the barracks was easy to find because it was the one with the music coming from behind the door. Ronan had heard him humming during workouts and while walking the halls. Something catchy and rhythmic, like an old tribal sort of song. Soulful.

Not sad, like the old children's song Tatima had been humming in her cell.

Ronan tapped on the door and then knocked a little louder when no answer came. The humming stopped, followed by a pause and a click. The door opened.

Noah answered, wearing nothing but pants. "Hey, man. Missed you at lunch. Heard you had family leave or something."

Ronan nodded. "Yeah. I'll be gone soon. Can I come in?"

Noah glanced up and down but stepped back. Hanging out in each other's rooms wasn't done, but not against the rules. The guards weren't buddies too often around here. He turned when he'd closed the door. "What's going on, friend?"

Ronan's blood pressure spiked nice and high. He stood on the brink of a huge gamble, but then, he'd already taken one. Fuck, he'd already taken enough that he was running out of fingers to count them. For that matter, he didn't know when his luck might change.

Ronan hoped he had one more good coin toss. "You made a comment one day at lunch, about how maybe the supernaturals aren't all bad. Did you mean what you said?"

Noah crossed his arms over his chest, every visible muscle tight in the man's body. That was a shit-ton of muscles. His shrewd eyes narrowed as he looked Ronan up and down. "Why?"

Ronan drew a deep breath. "I think someone who's in here shouldn't be. I want to take her with me when I leave."

Noah's head angled to the side. They stared each other down for so long, Ronan was sure his lungs would explode.

Until finally Noah's lips quirked into a small smile. "Man, you must be crazy"

As tall as Ronan was, he had to look up to make eye contact. He took a huge breath. "I'm pretty sure I am."

Noah's smile vanished as fast as it'd appeared. So fast, Ronan wondered if he'd imagined things. He gripped the straps of his duffel so tightly his fingers tingled. His heels lifted, ready to run if Noah went for his radio.

Plan B looked even messier and more dangerous when he'd sketched it out on the pages of his journal, but he'd go through all the letters of the alphabet until he came up with a way out. Or until he failed.

Noah took a step. Another. His hand reached, fingers opened, toward the low dresser on his right. Some clothes and socks sat stacked on top. So did a stun want and a comm device.

Ronan took a step back. One hand grabbed the knob on the door.

"Gonna get your ass killed," Noah murmured. He snatched a shirt from the top of the dresser and threw it on over his head.

"Probably." Ronan's lungs unlocked. He tried to ignore the ball of lead that lay in his stomach.

"The west perimeter is the least heavily guarded. Nothing past that wall except what remains of the North Woods."

"Uh-huh." Hot relief flooded Ronan's insides, but it was short lived once his head cleared. "No exit along that wall, either." A battle waged in his chest. Noah's information indicated a willingness to help. Except, it really wasn't help.

Noah sniffed quietly, bringing himself up to Ronan so they stood nearly chest to chest. "You know, my sister loved that guy. He *was* good to her. After the conservatives tried to quarantine the folks they went to the trouble of mucking around with and the new laws were passed, he was grabbed by some fear mongers and dragged behind a truck until he died. Horrible way to go. My sister was pregnant. She had it terminated because if she'd been found out having a half-breed, it would have been taken from her for testing. It was that or try to escape to the Western States, but she was afraid she wouldn't make it safely. Said she couldn't see putting an innocent child through all that torture. Three months later, she committed suicide. Her vehicle versus a stone wall."

God, that's awful. "I don't— I'm sorry." Every time Ronan thought he'd heard the worst of what went on in the world, the world upped the ante.

He had to get out of this place. "Why are you working here? Helping?"

Noah smiled slowly. "My man. You aren't the only one making plans." He took a step back. "Now if a person were trying to escape, there's a spot on that west perimeter that's been patched with old chain link, due to an errant weapons discharge shortly after my arrival. I seem to recall they haven't gotten around to putting any razor wire on top yet." He sobered. "Still. You'd have to get past me, since I guard that section. Once you're out there in those woods, it's all a gamble. Nothing but frozen and desolate for miles, buddy."

Ronan nodded. They were taking the longest of long shots but it was all they had.

He clasped Noah's hand. "Thank you."

"Don't thank me for handing over an early ticket to your funeral."

He smiled and turned for the door. "Then thank you for helping me do some damage on the way out."

Chapter Ten

Journal entry: 10.18.2668 (Nightfall)
  Okay:
  - mini torch
  - blankets
  - starter gel
  - duffel
  - clothing
  - energy bars
  - axe
  - ~~sanity~~
  - medPak
  Mom and Dad, if you're up there, help us out. Please.

***

Stealing the axe had been the biggest risk. The food, blankets, and medical items now stored in his duffel followed a close second, but those he had taken from the emergency supply closet on the ground floor. Not a frequently visited location. The axe, on the other hand, had come straight off the wall by the emergency power station.

Since the building used gas, they took fires seriously at the outpost. Ronan spent all afternoon and evening waiting for someone to notice that missing tool. If they had, they hadn't traced it back to him. Not yet.

Now though, it was go-time, and somebody was going to know. A lot of somebodies.

He decided to set up the fire near the kitchen and laundry services, on the minimum security ward. In part because it was an easy place. This time of evening, the staff had finished up and cleared out, and lots of shit there was flammable. Bigger bonus, it lay down the far arm of the compound, in the opposite direction of Ronan's target path. Draw them away, that was the goal.

He'd managed to snag five fire-starter packs. He saved two for just in case and stowed two under a laundry pile. He lit those, and then lit another, tossing it into a rolling dumpster of waste. With luck, that one would make lots of smoke.

He was heading out when the door clanged open. "Hey, what's that smell?"

"Some kind of smoke?"

"Better call maintenance."

Crouched behind a two-ton laundry bin, Ronan risked a glance to gauge the position of the two guards who'd entered, then pushed.

"What the fuck?"

"Shit. Move!"

Guard one didn't act fast enough. He tried to slide sideways as the bin came down but was rewarded with a blow to the head by the edge of the giant container.

Fuck, you've just signed yourself up for a cell next to Tatima's if this doesn't work.

He had no time to consider the body on the floor or wonder about its fate because the other guard came at him with a large hook used for disconnecting the hoses at the back of the industrial machines, and Ronan was forced to duck before his head wound up cracked and bleeding like the guy on the floor.

The guard growled. "What the fuck are you doing in here? Are you fucking insane?"

When the hook swung again, Ronan caught the metal pole it was attached to on the return. "Yeah," he growled. "I am definitely completely nuts." He jerked hard, pulling the pole and the guard both closer, and planted a boot in the guy's chest. With a shove he sent his opponent reeling against a table for folding clothes, and didn't think before he brought the hook down on the other man's head.

The room fell silent.

"Fuck, that's a lot of blood," Ronan whispered.

A quick pulse check assured him that he hadn't killed anyone, but neither man was in good shape. Head wounds always looked ugly. He had no time to stay and find out more. A pang of guilt hit him, but he turned away and tamped it down.

If I hadn't, I'd be the one there on the ground.

Ronan checked the laundry pile where he'd started his packets smoldering to be sure they were doing their thing, grabbed his bag, and raced out the door. He passed a control closet similar to the one they'd had on the max ward. He scanned his hand to see if he had access. Lucky thing: they'd keyed him in for this one already. Or he'd been programmed still from before.

He pulled out the ax, smashing the power panel once, twice, and with the third was finally gratified to get a spark. "Fuck, yes." He spun, making tracks down the hall. When he reached the end, he pulled the alarm. The breath in his chest seared on its way down as he bolted toward solitary confinement.

The same guard stood when he reached Tatima's cell. "Back again? Listen, they just called an alarm. I can't let you—"

Ronan elbowed the guard in the head. No time for persuasion. "Sorry," he muttered. He pulled the groggy young man up by the arm so he could use his hand scan to unlock Tatima's cell, then knocked his skull on the concrete one more time to ensure he'd stay out for a while.

Hell. This better work.

Last time he'd entered the cell, Tatima had been curled in a ball, injured and defeated. He expected to find her much the same way. Even so, he entered the cell cautiously, already unzipping his pack to find the spare sweats he'd scavenged for her.

She flew at him.

"Shit!" He dodged, forced to pull her arms behind him as if he might cuff her, but he didn't. He didn't want to, and he knew from past experience it wouldn't matter. "Have you lost your mind?"

Maybe Ronan needed to look hard in the mirror when he asked that question. His temperature spiked and sweat poured from his body. Jesus, he'd done all this to help her, and she was attacking him.

Don't forget you're also doing this for yourself.

Yes, but not entirely. Ronan wanted to get to his father's company. Find information and confront Fairfield. Still, escaping would have come with far less risk and a lower body count had he not been trying to release Tatima.

She hissed and turned, stronger than she'd been before. Thanks to him, more than likely. His blood—he'd healed her and made her strong. He knew it made them stronger, that's why they weren't allowed any blood in lockup. Ronan had broken that rule. He's broken so many.

Tatima squirmed in his grasp, nearly knocking his jaw off with the bottom of her head. "You. Cannot. Have. Me."

Dammit, she thought he'd come to hurt her.

Ronan's fury burned white-hot at the knowledge. How many had tried to take advantage? He didn't want to be in the same group as those men.

"Tatima, I'm here to help." He didn't want to have to hold her down, but he needed her to listen right fucking now. He caught her shoulders again—*damn, she's strong*—he tried to keep focused on her eyes. "I'm trying to get us both out, but we have to hurry. I need you with me."

She drew a gasp. "Ronan?" Her eyes widened. Recognition seemed to finally land in their depths. "What are you doing? How?"

She tried to back away, but he held on to her shoulders. "I'm getting us *out*. As fast as fucking possible. I have clothes. I'll get them out if you promise not to come at me again when I let go."

She nodded like she understood. They were both dead if she didn't.

"Here. Hurry." He handed over a shirt and pants he'd grabbed in the laundry area and zipped his pack. He'd found a spare flak vest as well, which he helped her put on. "Come on, we have to go." He peeked through the cracked-open cell door into the hall to find the guard groaning on the floor. "Now."

She took his hand when he offered, even though she looked at him like she was still confused. "Why are you doing this?"

"You need to get to your son. I need answers from Fairfield. If he killed my father, he needs to be held accountable. Are you coming?"

They ran. Out the door at the rear of the compound and along the back wall. "Weave," he told her. "Make it hard for them to shoot us. Go for the open spot on the fence." But he held her hand so they had to stay connected. He wanted to ensure they both made it over the wall.

Noah met them at the far corner of the yard, and other footsteps weren't far behind. "Let's see what you got, friend."

Ronan punched him in the nose, then reached for his shoulders and put a knee in his balls.

"Ass...hole."

Ronan bent down. "Better if I put you on the ground, right? Looks real."

The big man groaned. "Yeah. Perfect. Nothing says conspiracy like you leaving my nuts intact." He reached to clasp Ronan's hand. "Good luck."

When Ronan pulled away there was a key in his hand. He looked at Noah. "What's this?"

"There's an old motorbike parked straight into the North Woods a few clicks. Won't be comfortable, but it'll get you on your way."

"What about you?" They couldn't leave Noah stranded here. God only knew what would happen if someone realized Noah was a traitor. Why would he make this sacrifice for them?

Footsteps got louder. Shots fired.

Tatima ran toward the fence. "Ronan!"

Noah jerked his chin. "I'm okay. Go."

So they went.

Chapter Eleven

Journal entry:10.19.2668

I can't believe she's sleeping. That she trusted me enough to keep watch after the sun rose. Or maybe she was simply too exhausted.

I don't know how I'll repay Noah. If we'll even see him again.

I don't even know what his game is, but we found the motorbike he left. There was a map of the old logging roads hidden under the seat. Spots were marked that I think must have been places he'd scouted to hide out, because it led us to this abandoned cabin left over from before the local water dried up.

A handful of ancient trees still stand, but not many. It's cool looking, in an eerie way, or it would be if we weren't busy being fugitives.

According to Tatima, they have more trees in the Western States, where there's still plentiful water. She's heard of others escaping over the border, where supernaturals have freedom. We talked briefly about getting her across since her parents were lost during the rebellion. It's a hike, but by far the safest place.

Still, we can't leave the Eastern States without going back to my father's company to find her son. I need to go, too.

I'm hoping we'll find answers.

It's a good thing I'm right handed, since my left arm isn't good for much right now. I got bit in the back of the shoulder with a bullet I can't remove. Hopefully when Tatima wakes she can help.

God. Already, I'm counting on her, and that's dangerous. I don't even know how long we'll stick together.

I guess I still don't know for sure if I can trust her, but I can admit at least on paper that I want to. Watching her now, she looks like the girl I remember. She looks... peaceful. Her nose is sort of turned upward, and her lips are pouty and open partway. Once in a while I hear a soft snore, and I'm actually glad. This is probably the first decent rest she's gotten in some time.

This cabin isn't much. It's tiny and dirty, and empty except for some old trash and dead leaves. We're sleeping on the thin blankets I stole. It's freezing, but it's shelter. We're safe for the time being.

I want to get close to her because she's warm and soft, but every time I do alarms trip all over my brain. We don't have the same familiarity we once did, and a brief kiss is a long way from wrapping my body around hers.

We are supposed to be enemies. Right now, I'm still the one with more power because of the daylight. I can't simply lay my body down against hers without permission.

I want to, though. I remember holding her close in that solitary cell, and I crave the heat and solid reassurance of her. Right or wrong, I can't deny she fit nicely in my arms. Still, it wouldn't be right.

I'm not supposed to want to. What if I find out she's lied this whole time, and the woman I'm feelings these things for is a monster?

The more I think of what I learned, the more I believe that sweet executive assistant I knew has got to still be in there. Looking at her now? She seems the same, only older and more weary.

So am I.

I watch her sleep, and for once in my life, I have hope. Hope that I've done something good.

***

"You're bleeding."

Ronan took a pause from stuffing supplies into his bag. He bit the supplement bar in his throbbing hand and chewed slowly before he replied. "No big deal." Really, it burned worse than a flesh-eating wasp sting. He couldn't entirely explain to himself why he didn't want her to worry.

"Let me help."

Ronan stiffened before he nodded. He'd accepted that he'd need her help, but what trust they had skated on a thin sheet of newly formed ice. There he sat, about to turn his back on her and hand her something sharp.

Pointing to a spot in the corner, he said, "I've laid out tweezers and a bandage already. I tried but I couldn't reach it myself. If you could—"

"If I gave you my blood it would heal fast."

His head nearly twisted off his shoulders. "What?"

She still lay on her side under the blankets, eyes half-lidded from sleep. "My blood. It heals. What do you think those experiments were about? The government was looking for a new biological whatever-you-call-it. You worked in that same lab once, didn't you? You should know."

Ronan turned back around. "I'm not going to take advantage of some government-sponsored experiment my father's company did on you." He shook his head. "Anyway, could be dangerous." Humans weren't meant to drink blood.

He didn't realize Tatima had left the makeshift bed until the pads of her fingers carefully explored around his wound. "I wouldn't have suggested something dangerous. You know there was human testing. Soldiers, mostly. Wounded in battle." Hurt and grief seemed to echo in her words. "The wound isn't deep. It would heal in minutes." Her exhale sent tingles across the back of his neck. "You did the same thing for me."

He frowned. "Just take it out with the tweezers. Please."

She sighed and picked up the tools. "We're going with slow and painful, then. You're in charge."

Ronan gritted his teeth. "Are you willing to tell me what happened when you were there? At the lab?"

Her hair brushed his back, and her breath caressed his skin. Neither of them moved. Finally, she said, "Like I told you, they said it was a drug testing program. I needed money. I think that's how so many of us got in there. They had a lot of students. They kept us in the dark about what they were doing. I started to suspect, but we'd signed a contract that if we didn't go through with the whole thing, we didn't get our money."

Silence followed, then a long sigh. "I tried to get out of it, the way I told you."

"The technician you mentioned?"

"Yes. Either he screwed up or he lied. Either way, it only created a bigger nightmare. I love my son, but I would never have knowingly brought a child into that life. They let us go briefly, but thanks to that ugly rebellion they rounded us all up again."

"Probably because the rebellion had started, and you guys were proof that the lab had been doing things they shouldn't."

"Whatever the reason, they had a field day with me because I was pregnant. They drew a lot of blood. They ran tests. Tried to determine how much damage we could handle before we couldn't regenerate, which was the only test I got out of. " She breathed a bitter laugh. "They didn't want to cause me stress. Because I was expecting. As if seeing the others go through it wasn't stressful."

Whether she realized it or not, Tatima's fingers dug into Ronan's shoulder. He put a hand over hers. He wasn't sure what else to say or do.

Ronan could imagine what the sorts of tests she described might entail, and that picture turned his stomach. He didn't realize he'd laced their fingers together until her hand twitched against his. "I'm sorry." He cleared his throat. "Go ahead. If you're... If you don't mind."

She sighed, squeezing the hand on his shoulder. "Some of us tried to escape after the rebellion, but we didn't have rights anymore. Where was there to go? Your father was killed when Fairfield decided he needed to get rid of Freyenne. He'd taken her on as a 'special interest.' I was trying to help her escape when your father showed up." She sniffed. "He didn't work there every day anymore, but sometimes he stopped by to look around. Usually during the lunch hour, so I think his visit was unexpected. Fairfield meant to kill Freyenne so she attacked. Your father got in the way."

He digested her words, and they soured in his gut. "I didn't realize." God damn. "I was off sticking my head in the dirt. I heard things about dealing with the supernatural problem. I didn't pay attention, because I thought it didn't concern me."

He tried to turn and face her but her hand touched his cheek. "Stop, I need to see what's going on back here. Anyway, it's... It happened. What matters in these situations is how we survive. *If* we survive," she whispered

Ronan's heart grew heavier with the weight of her observation. They were on the run in the freezing middle of nowhere. They'd been discovered missing by now. Survival certainly looked iffy. "We will do better than survive," he said. "We'll go back and tear that lab apart."

One of them had to be sure. If he voiced doubt, they'd never live.

She prodded at the wound with her fingers. "This doesn't look good. It grosses you out, drinking my blood?"

"No!" He stood and reached for the supplies. "Look, never mind. I'll get it out myself."

"Stop. I was only trying to examine our options. You helped me, so let me help you." She pushed off the blanket and half crawled over. "Sit." Her hand pressed against his already bare shoulder.

He closed his mouth and breathed in and out. While she grabbed an alcohol pad and gently wiped it over the wound, her breath tickled his neck again. Ronan tried to tell himself he only shivered because the North Woods were colder than Odin's dick.

"Your skin is like ice." She pressed herself against Ronan's back, sliding her arms along his.

Warmth built inside of him, traveling through his body and gathering in his core. "What are you doing? How can you do that?"

"My body temperature is usually higher others'. I make for a good furnace when I'm healthy." She pressed further. Her silky hair slid over his shoulders. Her breasts brushed against him through her shirt. Her belly molded to his lower back. Her lips feathered against his ear. "This brave prison guard let me drink from him, and I'm stronger than I've been in months." She squeezed his good shoulder. "Thank you."

"You're— *Fuck!*" Searing pain shot through his shoulder to his arm, his back, and his neck. He clamped his teeth together.

"Ah. There it is. Told you I'd help." Tatima held her bloody fingers in front of him, bullet pinched between her thumb and forefinger. "Funny that such a small thing can cause so much pain Okay, give me the bandage." She dropped the bullet on the floor and covered the wound with a light touch. "Nothing I can stitch you up with?"

He shook his head. "That stuff's hard to come by without raiding the medical unit."

Her hair brushed his shoulder again as she pressed the gauze over his wound. "You know, I'm told it tastes surprisingly good to humans. Our blood, I mean."

He looked over his shoulder in time to see the ghost of hurt on her face. "I didn't mean to offend you. I just think it's better if I don't." He didn't know what would happen if he consumed her blood. He'd heard things. Ugly things. Probably false things, but caution seemed prudent.

Besides, after the experience of giving her *his* blood, it sounded oddly intimate. They were free of the outpost, but in a way he still held most of the cards. Especially since she had to remain with him for safety during the daylight. He needed emotional distance for the sake of his sanity. "I'm trying to be professional here, Tatima. Enough people have taken advantage of you. I don't want to be another one who takes."

Something like hurt scrawled itself across her face. "Do you call resting your forehead against mine and putting your hands in my hair when I'm naked in a cell 'professional,' Ronan?"

Shame and anger erupted from deep inside. He jerked away, his hands clenched. "I did my best to help you without taking advantage. You know damn well that's true."

Her face fell. "You did. I'm sorry. You've been better to me than anybody since this nightmare started, and it's not like you were a stranger. I don't always handle all this stress so well. I know you're trying to help."

"I sure as hell hope so."

She smiled. "Let's get cleaned up, and I suggest we huddle together for warmth until it's safe to move again. You're no good to me if you're frozen."

Ronan managed to smile. He took in the answering upturn in her lips, still feeling the heat and softness of her fingers on his skin even though he'd withdrawn from her touch. She really did seem to have a gentle spirit. Her smile, the way she'd cared for him just then.

Ronan had just been sitting with his shirt off and his back to Tatima in a cold room, while he trusted her to remove a bullet from him. She could have killed him, if she'd been the kind who would. She hadn't.

Maybe she needs your help to get to the border.

Ronan shook away the arguing voices and pulled his shirt back on over his head. "Okay. While we're keeping each other warm, perhaps you could tell me anything more you know about my father. We weren't close the last couple of years, and I'd be appreciative"

She surprised him by turning to kiss his cheek. "I didn't know him well either, but I'll gladly tell you what I can."

They wrapped themselves up in the blankets. Tatima surprised Ronan by wiggling closer until her back met his front, and pulling his arm around her waist.

Ronan relaxed as her heat melted into his skin, and tried not to like the feel of her against him too much.

Chapter Twelve

Journal entry: 10.19.2668

We're tired and disoriented from zig-zagging through the woods. It's tough, because I want to conserve our gas and I want to keep to the old logging roads so I can maintain my bearings. I also want to confuse anybody who might be on our trail.

It's also tough because Tatima has been plastered against me for hours. Except for the fast-as-possible stops we've made, she's had her front to my back, her arms around my waist, and her thighs squeezing my hips for enough teeth-chattering hours that it's hard to remember my own name.

We finally stopped to rest and stretch our legs. I found one of those old-style tractor trailers that had been abandoned, with a bed in the back and everything. Big time dusty in there, but otherwise okay. I'm not convinced we'd make it to the next spot on Noah's map by daybreak. She says she can take some sunlight if she has to, but I want to save trying something like that for an emergency.

I wonder if Noah's okay. I'm grateful to him for helping. This little bike moves surprisingly fast. Tomorrow we'll be outside of Boston if we can maintain our pace. On foot I doubt we'd have survived.

***

Tatima listened to the crush of quiet surrounding them in the woods, now that Ronan's blood had sharpened her hearing. She hated to admit the relief at having her senses working properly again. The dull ringing in her ears, the buzz in her head—being weakened in that detention center had left her disoriented and added to her fear.

Now, with the exception of some lingering nausea, she had control of her body. Thanks to Ronan. It seemed so surreal, but the proof ran in her veins.

"You can take the bed." Ronan scanned the area around them. He'd been looking here and there for food each time they stopped. Little in the way of woodland animals these days though, and less of things like edible fruits and berries. He stretched his neck and back, probably stiff from all the hours of clutching the handlebars of a motorbike. He looked like his shoulder hurt, and his movements took effort. "I'll stretch across the front seat of the truck cab."

He winced when he pulled at the rusted door of the truck. Tatima put her hand on his arm, and he went still.

"Let me," she said. Under her force, the door opened almost with little effort, and heat rose to her face. Showing him up would do no good, but neither would letting him cause himself further damage.

"It's a tradeoff, you know." She toed at the hard ground beneath them. "When they first did this to me, I got so angry at being unable to see the sun. I'd hear the humans around me say simple things like 'it's such a gorgeous day today' and be practically in tears. But at least I'm strong." She smiled at him, trying to let him know she acknowledged what he'd done for her. "When I'm fed, anyway."

He glanced up at the sky. It had turned a lighter shade of gray, but dawn had not yet fully broken through the trees. "You said you could withstand some sun. You know because you've tried?"

"A girl always has to try." Even as the memory scorched her skin, she tried to turn her smile playful to break through the tension hanging over both of their heads. "I'm sorry, by the way." She wrapped her fingers around his forearm. The gesture was meant to be simple, something to re-enforce her words, but the sturdy familiarity of his arm anchored her more than it should have.

He'd done what she needed him to do. Now free of the outpost, they could have gone their separate ways. Still, getting into his father's company would be easier with him along.

Those all worked as viable excuses. It didn't hurt that Ronan had been kind to her, and she'd had little enough that she'd take that where she could. Not simply kind, but gentle. She'd liked the way his hands and cheek had laid comfortingly against her skin, without pushing or pulling or asking for more.

It didn't hurt that he reminded her of who she was... before.

"What are you apologizing to me for?" He twitched like he might pull away, but didn't.

She smiled again. The woods were cold, and riding that bike with the wind whipping past them, even colder. They'd both be smart to seek each other's warmth. Each other's comfort.

"I'm not sure, but I feel like I made you angry." She frowned. "I wasn't trying to push it on you. My blood." She wrapped her other arm around herself, blocking some of the chill.

He'd opened up some in the cabin, but his face looked darker now, more like he had when they met early on at the outpost. Tatima wanted the friendly version of Ronan back. "I know you put a lot on the line for me," she said. "I feel like the only thing I have to give in return is a part of me."

The horrified expression on his face told her she'd said the wrong thing.

"Which is one very important reason why I can't accept." He wouldn't look her in the eye now. Instead he gazed up at the lightening sky again. He pulled the blanket from his pack, handing it and his jacket to her. "Come on. The sun is rising, and I don't want to test your theories about the sunlight unless it's necessary. Let's get some rest."

He'd turned for the other door, but Tatima caught Ronan's hand in both of hers. "It's freezing out here, Ronan. We both need a decent day's rest, and who knows when we'll get another chance at a real bed? I think we can be adult enough to share body heat, don't you? We managed before."

She held her breath in her throat, staring into his coal-dark eyes while she waited for him to either turn her away or—the faded moon willing—take her by the hand and accept the warmth she wanted to share with him.

Tatima had been forced to endure many things. This man in front of her who had once kissed her as if she might run away from fright, this man was the only one who had refused to take advantage of her helplessness. She wasn't helpless any longer.

"Come on, Ronan." She pulled him inside the cab with a smile. One strand of her hair slipped over her shoulder and he brushed it from her face with a shaky finger.

"I can't..."

I missed feeling connected to him like this. Like I did the day he kissed me. He doesn't want to, but he wants to be close to me as much as I want to be close to him. Maybe I shouldn't want him, either, but he's familiar and handsome and he's a good guy. When did I last have anything good?

Tatima licked her lips. "How tall would you say you are? Six feet?"

Ronan swallowed. "Six-one."

She put one hand to his shoulder, pressing him to the thin mattress. "How much do you weigh?"

"One ninety-five."

Tatima's hand pushed harder. She held Ronan's gaze and let it calm the rush of her blood, the sharp hammer of her heart.

She leaned close, not quite bumping their noses again. "You've got five inches and plenty of pounds on me," she whispered. "Now get up. Walk away."

"What?"

"Go on. Here, I'm only pushing with one hand."

Ronan lifted his shoulders, and his grimace showed she'd made her point. "I get it. You're strong."

"I am now. The truth is, now that I'm powered up and we're out of that place I could leave you any time I wanted. If you don't want to be with me, I'll understand. If it's fairness you're worried about, I want you to realize you can't do anything without my consent. Not now." She ran her hand along his jaw. "We're a threat to normal humans because when we're fed and healthy, we are stronger than any of you. They handle the fear by keeping us weak and contained."

"I'm not afr—" He stopped the denial before he finished the lie. And she knew it was one. They both did.

"You *were*. You thought I killed your father."

His head dropped back. "I didn't want to believe you were capable, but your name was in all the papers. And I so wanted someone to blame."

Her hands slid into the collar of his shirt, popping one button and then another. "And now?" The air grew thick around them, their breath so heavy it fogged in the small space. They should be running, hating each other, even both at the same time.

The illicitness made Tatima's blood rush faster.

Ronan nodded. "I couldn't..." Static electricity charged in the air. He opened and closed his mouth like he wasn't sure what to say. "My father trusted you once. So did I. I'd like to think neither of us were stupid. You never felt dangerous. The things you said resonated..." he tapped his chest with his hand. "I still need to fill in a lot of holes, but from what info I was able to get, the stuff you told me was accurate. I didn't realize Fairfield had taken over my father's operations. Last I knew, he was a mid-level manager and a small-time politician. I don't know what he'd be doing overseeing the labs and everything."

Tatima wrinkled her nose. "He wasn't a good person. I didn't like him." Her other hand came to Ronan's chest, spreading open his uniform shirt.

His fists clenched and released, one hand coming up like he might try to push her away. "Tatima..."

She shivered. "I'll confess to you that I'm scared. So much I don't have the words. We don't know how this will end. We don't even know if we'll make it out alive. I hope so like crazy, but we don't know anything for sure." Tatima ran her hand over his short dark hair, tracing the back of his neck. The swirls of amber in his eyes pulled her forward. "You've been good to me, Ronan. I can't erase the awful things I've experienced, but it would be nice to have one day of memories that matter out here."

Ronan's only answer was a heavy flood of breath, and his large hands wrapping around either side of her waist as she knelt beside him.

Tatima stretched one leg across his lap. His erection pressed, large and insistent between her legs, as if seeking her heat. A strange sense of power gripped Tatima. She smiled down at Ronan and planted one hand on either side of his chest. "You're not answering. Should I stop?"

Ronan tightened his hands. "Everything I've been told says this is wrong."

She couldn't deny the truth of his words, even though they shot a barbed spear into her center. Adrenaline and nerves made her shudder. "Because of your training? The criminal code? By that logic, we shouldn't be here at all. I should be in a cell. You should still be putting poison in my water."

An angry-sounding hiss escaped from between his teeth "Fuck. You're right." Ronan's hands tangled in her hair. He pulled her head to his and their lips met, hot and furious.

Tatima eased back for a few breaths to put her hands over his. Even in these sweaty, staccato kisses, she could tell he held himself back. "Stop thinking so hard. We don't know if we have a tomorrow, Ronan. Just feel."

Ronan ran his hands over her back, so slowly that his fingertips woke up the flesh underneath. "I do feel. Your skin is the softest thing I've ever touched."

His mouth tasted like heat and certainty. Fire blazed through Tatima, igniting in a bright blaze when the tip of his tongue touched hers. White-hot flames licked her arms when he unclenched his hands and skimmed them up to her shoulders. They fanned across her back, digging in and kneading with tiny circles.

"I can't believe I'm touching you." Ronan's face reflected his surprise. He pulled his hands away and then scowled at them like they were naughty children who had been doing something they shouldn't have without his permission.

He squeezed his eyes shut, his chest rising and falling. "Sorry. It's been a while," he whispered.

Tatima shifted on top of him, smiling. He was trying to be gentle. To let her take control. Something swelled inside of her, something she couldn't describe with words.

She still couldn't quite reconcile this young man with the one who'd stared at her with vengeful eyes when she'd first seen him at North Woods. Best if she stopped trying. Tatima pulled off her shirt and immediately sought his warmth. .

Ronan opened his eyes. "Fucking beautiful." His hand hovered at the small of her back. "Can I touch you?"

She pushed his shirt aside. "Only if I can take off your pants," she whispered.

Ronan's eyes crinkled at the corners when he grinned back. Maybe the first time she'd seen him genuinely express pleasure. He lifted his hips to help while she relieved him of pants and underwear, still drinking in his face. She laid herself across his body, arms and legs wrapped around him. "It's cold. Keep me warm."

He went along with the obvious ploy, running his hands across her shoulders, her arms, her back. Both of them gasped when he teased the right spot below her navel. He seemed as delighted by pleasing her as he was surprised that he was able to.

She'd pulled off the rest of her clothing and lifted herself above him, and he groaned again. "I've never seen anything hotter."

Heat flooded Tatima's body. "You really think I'm pretty?"

"No." Ronan ran a hand over her stomach, between her breasts, and around the back of her neck. "I think you're gorgeous. I hope I can make you feel nearly as good as you look."

She had to kiss him. Had to. If she found out he was lying tomorrow, she'd take it. Right then she believed him, and nobody had ever made her feel pretty in a way that felt this honest.

He stopped her when she shifted lower. "I don't have anything to use for protection."

She pushed away a shadow of sadness as she traced a path down his chest with her finger. "I can't conceive again, and there's not much else you might catch from me, except the pox." Which wasn't transmitted that way, anyway.

She leaned close, brushing her hands, her hair, and her breasts all over Ronan's to get him distracted so he wouldn't ask more questions. "You know, it's so frigid out here in these woods," she whispered. "Especially for a human. Let's get you warm."

Ronan didn't say no when her mouth closed over his. "Funny, I'm warmer already."

Then, he was inside her.

As they moved together, she used her heightened senses to listen to the woods in case any danger came near. The rest of her got lost in the brush of skin against skin, the wide eyes staring up at her and the glow of his smile. The heave of his breath as she rode him like they might not have a tomorrow.

Because they might not. "Tatima." He breathed her name into the morning mist and thrust upward, and she tightened her legs around him. Excitement and desire wound through her and fed the gathering storm in her core.

God, it had been so long.

"Ronan." She dug her fingers into his shoulders. "Please."

She sped up, fangs extended. Her nails sank deeper into his shoulders. She wasn't used to asking for what she wanted. With him though, it made sense.

Tatima took hold of his hand and moved it to her back. "Scratch me." She'd never wanted this before. This one time, she needed to feel alive. She pulled his fingers to her lips, sucking one and then two fingers into her mouth. "Ronan... Please..."

"Yes." He gripped the fleshy part of her hip with his free hand and dug in with his nails, giving her a small bite of pain. Only enough to pierce the pleasure.

In kind, Tatima nipped the tips of Ronan's fingers with her fang. She sucked the tiny bead of blood, snaking her tongue around each digit, gratified at the way it spurred him to gasp and thrust harder from beneath. "I can't believe this. I want..." She laced her fingers over Ronan's, holding the pulse in his wrist against her lips.

In that moment she rode the edge of a fierce storm in the arms of a man who was supposed be her enemy, and it was *everything*. "Yes," he whispered again.

Wave after wave, they moved together. Their faces pressed, sharing heated breath and urgent pleasure.

In a human's blink she'd pierced the flesh of his wrist and begun to drink. With her first suck Ronan dug his fingers into her back, arching upward.

A fierce growl ripped from his lips as his release pulsed inside her.

Tatima stared down as her release shattered her, marveling at a connection that made sense even though it was one she didn't understand. Her fangs piercing his skin, his nails piercing hers. Pain. Pleasure.

A circle.

He smiled, his eyes glazed but staring up at her with apparent satisfaction. He ran a strand of her hair between his fingers. "That was amazing."

"It was." Awareness hit her with a sudden chill. There she was, naked and freezing, and in a truck with her jailer. What was she doing?

Yes, she knew Ronan, but parts of this felt too familiar once the fog of her desire had cleared.

"Hey. Don't." His hand found hers. "You said no thinking, right? That we needed to find some good. You were right. Was it good?"

She shivered from the cold. "Yes. I'm sorry. I'm..."

"I know. So am I. We're going to figure it out."

"I hope so." She curled into him. It *had* been good. Then the euphoria had cleared from her brain and she was still too far from her son. Perhaps too far from her right mind.

He helped her pull her shirt over her head. "Okay. Let's keep each other warm, like you suggested. Let's get some actual sleep. If things still seem awful at nightfall, I'll apologize."

"It was my idea." Now he was trying to make her feel better for a problem she'd created, and she felt even worse.

He smiled slightly. "Then you'll apologize."

She pulled her pants on and took a breath, wrapping around him. "That almost sounded like a joke. I haven't heard you tell one since I saw you at the outpost. You used to be so funny, before. Is this okay?"

"Is it okay with you?"

"Yes. I don't—"

"Stop. It's okay." He closed his eyes and pulled her close. "This is scary shit. Like you said, we don't know what's coming. So let's take what we can get. For all I know, you're plotting my death. But you were kind enough to wring me out first, so it'll be a good way to go." He placed a gentle kiss on the side of her head.

She managed a slight chuckle. "Courtesy sex. You're right. I've trusted the wrong humans too many times. It's made me nervous."

"I don't trust easily either. I'll be here, though, if you change your mind."

Tatima grabbed Ronan's hand. "I'm simply not used to feeling this way, you know? I don't trust it."

"And what way is that," he murmured against her neck.

"Good."

Chapter Thirteen

Journal entry: 10.22.2668

I woke with my lips pressed to the back of Tatima's neck and my arm encircling her waist. She made these little noises and squirmed closer to me when I moved, and I wished we could stay that way until the world ended. Probably the first time in my life I've wished to go back to sleep.

Impossible for so many reasons. I wonder if I'm only feeling this because of the young love I thought I'd buried or because we're compressed into this situation together. I wonder how I can know for sure.

Noises in the surrounding woods made me slip out around midday. I didn't want an attack forcing Tatima into the daylight. It turned out to be a couple and their child, heading north in hopes of getting over the Canadian border, one of the places where supernaturals have rights. She was a siren-type, and he had been a logger before the business dried up. Their son—teenaged, maybe—seemed fine. Like a normal kid, not mutated the way we'd heard stories. Half-breeds carried volatile DNA according to the "literature." The more I think about all the things I've been taught, the more I think it's all lies.

I hope it's all lies.

The couple was nice. They traded me some jerky for my extra Buzzer, which I hated to part with, but they were out here without much in the way of weapons. And the kid gave me this nice drawing he'd done of a mule deer. Apparently there are still a few out in these woods. And squirrels. Nothing kills them, I guess. Everything is starving, so if you put some food down, they'll come. I think later I may try to—

***

"What are you doing?"

Ronan snapped the journal closed and stowed it in his pack before she had a chance to read over his shoulder. "Didn't mean to wake you. Sorry."

Her head came over his shoulder. "What are you writing?"

He tried to move, but there wasn't room in the cab to get away without hitting a wall or leaving the small bunk, which he wasn't yet ready to do. He'd already had one taste of the freezing-cold weather. "It's nothing. I keep a journal."

"Oh." The frown eased from her face. "Okay."

He flipped onto his back so he could see her face. He'd used an emergency blanket to block out the window of the cab, but a little diffused evening light still filtered through the edges. Enough to see her golden skin and cobalt eyes. "I'm not writing a status report to my superiors or anything if that's what you think."

"I don't—" Her mouth shut abruptly. "I wondered why."

"I guess I always have, so I still do." But his chest burned at the pain on her face. He brought his palm to the place below where he'd seen the tattooed footprints on her body. He hovered there over her heart, not quite trusting himself to touch as she adjusted her clothes. "It's going to be okay."

Moisture leaked from her eyes. She didn't look away, so he didn't either. "It's hard to believe."

Her words wrapped around Ronan's heart and made it ache. "Are you sure he's being kept at my father's labs?" Ronan's fingers tightened, making a fist with an unfortunate lack of a target. He realized he shook inside at an injustice he couldn't claim total innocence from. In the privilege of his unaltered humanity, wasn't he in some way to blame?

"God, I hope so. If he isn't there, I don't know where to look." More tears rolled down her face. "Ronan, he's got to be so scared. I don't even know if he understands where I went."

"I snuck a look at your file. Your record said you'd tried to escape during transport."

Her head dipped slightly. "I had to try." Her tears flowed faster.

He realized their fingers were linked and wondered when it had happened. "I found things out that made me question everything, including whether you were telling the truth." He slid one of the Ellanol vials from his pack. "I told you not to drink the water in your cell because this is what was being used to poison you. All the prisoners on your ward. I helped as an assistant in the R&D lab when this was developed. It was supposed to help my mom but it sped her death. I don't know why it's still being used for anything at all."

Her face got cloudy. "Where did you get those?"

"I took them instead of dumping them into the water supply."

Her small gasp was followed by a kiss so light and quick Ronan almost wondered if he'd imagined it. The evening chill blew a breeze that picked up the extra moisture on his lips, so it must have been real. "What was that for?" He gripped her arms, wanting to pull her to him and do it more.

"A thank you. It's a relief, you know? That we're away from the ugliness of that place." She sighed something that sounded like frustration and leaned across him, placing a hand on his chest. "I understand what you said before, and I appreciate your respect. I haven't been in too many situations lately where I get a choice, you know?"

His chest ached. He didn't know, at least not exactly. He could only imagine, and he was sure his imagination didn't come close. "I'm sorry."

It seemed he'd said those words so much. And that he couldn't say them enough.

She shook her head. "What I'm saying is I know that's not what happened between us. We're not back in that cell. We're out here in the cold together. Maybe it's even a little like when we both worked for your father. When we kissed." The statement came as her lips hovered so close to his. Her nose brushed against his, and the gentle motion sent a cascading shiver to every exposed nerve.

"I... yes. If you see it that way." His arm curled around her waist in the midst of his answer.

Her lips came down on his again. "It was my choice," she murmured. "I've had time to think. I know it was. And I'm glad."

He pulled her against him. He needed to feel her skin, and he couldn't stop this time.

"I can feel your blood stirring inside me," she whispered.

Ronan brought one arm around her shoulders, the other slipped down her back. The lingering mistrust in his heart slipped away like distant, wispy smoke in his mind. He could hardly remember it as he pulled her close. "This is okay?"

She bumped her nose against his. "I'm saying it is."

Ronan stilled when Tatima pressed her hand to his chest. He stared up into her cobalt eyes, lit from the rising moon like they contained magic. With two fingers he reached up and let a strand of her hair slide between them. The soft touch of her hair was addictive. "I can't get over how beautiful you are."

"I'm not."

"You are." He brushed his lips over hers before peeking at the falling dusk through the crack in the truck window. "Believe me. I want to show you now, all over again, how beautiful I think you are. Night is falling though, and we need to get moving. The sooner we get to Old Boston, the sooner we can find your son."

She kissed him again. "I still can't believe you're helping me."

Ronan tried to smile. "I can't believe there was ever any doubt." That he'd been bent on vengeance when she came into the outpost drove guilt deep into his gut.

He couldn't believe he'd considered the idea of killing her. Even if only briefly.

If she knew, she wouldn't be grateful. She'd hate him.

Chapter Fourteen

Entry:10.22.2668 (Tatima)

Ronan said he wrote in his little book in order to help him figure out things he couldn't say aloud to anyone. I decided I'd try. I tore a piece from the back of his, and I hope he won't mind.

The woods freeze to the bone out here, especially at night. Even for someone like me who has the benefit of an elevated body temperature. I worry for Ronan with his genetic weakness, sturdy and young though he is. His body fat is minimal and I wish now I'd taken less of his blood. I wish he'd let me give back his coat. He insists each time I try that I need it more.

I don't, but I'm touched.

I realize I'm struggling when it comes to him. Nothing is simple—when I caught his conflicted glances at me in the shower I hoped I could use his position and his male lust to my advantage to get back to my son. Maybe, God willing, to the coast or even to Canada where we could live free.

I told myself I would use Ronan and I would do so without remorse, because those in his position had hurt me and were the reason I'd landed on the freezing tip of nowhere. In spite of the fact that we'd met each other a lifetime ago, I didn't expect him to be caring. I didn't expect to like him this way.

We got lucky and found this cabin along the edge of a trail that was home to a sympathetic—a human supporter of supernaturals, marked by a wreath of twigs on the door. A man and his son, his wife had been taken, accused of being like me and then kidnapped. Never found. Now they help others in her memory.

It's not the first story I've heard of these false accusations and attacks. Why do they seem so often to take the women? Maybe they simply think we have less value. Or we're easier to take.

It's good of these people to have taken us in, knowing where we came from. This home is warm. Quiet and comfortable. The father, Charles, said we could stay awhile if we wished.

I almost do wish we could stay, but I need to get to my boy.

God, if you haven't burned up with the overheated sun, please take care of my Valo.

***

Ronan moaned when the first bite of stew hit his tongue. Flavors of venison, potato, and herbs he'd forgotten existed burst in his mouth. He nodded to Charles and Benjamin, the two older humans who had taken them in. "This is amazing. I haven't tasted anything like this since my mother was alive."

Ben, the younger of the two, smiled wide. "I cooked with my mother when I was young. She taught me all about getting the most from your food."

Ronan shoveled more soup into his mouth, grateful for the warmth. "But where do you get this food? Even as a guard, everything they gave us over at the outpost tasted like shit."

"We manage. Ain't easy, but we have a sunroom upstairs where we grow a few things, and when we feel we can risk it, we drive to a trading post. Once in a while folks offer a little something if they have it, in exchange for helping or for getting them over the border to safety." He put up his hands. "Not that I ask such a thing. No payment at all is required, and we are happy to help."

Ronan made a note to check his pack for things he might be able to leave as a token. They needed to head out of the woods and get on the main road, but this chance to rest, clean up, and get warm was a lifesaver.

He looked over toward the stairs, where Tatima had gone to bathe and lie down. He'd tried to wake her when the food came out but she'd been asleep in the small bed, one arm flopped over her head, drooling on the lumpy pillow. Wondering when she last slept so hard, Ronan couldn't bring himself to wake her.

"Leave her alone," Charles said. "She seemed troubled when you two arrived, and that's not something a man should poke his head into lightly. Besides, supernaturals don't need food like we do."

Ronan sucked down the rest of his meal, ignoring his unease. He could guess at what troubled Tatima—they were most likely being hunted, and God knew whether her son was okay—Ronan could do nothing for her but try to keep her safe and pray.

He'd stopped praying after his mother's death. After everything that had happened then, he and God shouldn't be speaking. If he couldn't say anything nice, after all.

Still, this wasn't for him. Praying couldn't hurt.

Ronan nodded at their hosts. "You might be right." He still wanted to see her. "We should probably go as soon as night falls, but is there anything I can do to help you while we're here?" Not sure if he had anything they could leave behind, the least they could do was try to offer service.

Charles nodded toward his son. "I've been after Benji here to shore up a crack in the wall of the food cellar. Couple odd jobs here and there. If you're willing to assist, we'd be grateful."

"Absolutely."

After their meal, Ronan followed Benjamin to a dark annex dug under the basement and roughly bricked over. This small place was nothing like the large home he'd grown up in, but he appreciated the cozy surroundings. These men had everything they needed.

"So it's this wall here," Benjamin said when they got downstairs. He gestured to an area around a door where the bricks had fallen from the wall.

"I haven't seen anything built with this old brick stuff in forever." Ronan reached out to touch the rough, rocklike material. Everything these days was built from cinderblock or steel. Nothing but gray covered the landscape. Wood came rotted or petrified if it came at all, and rock quarries didn't operate much any longer. The small brick hadn't been produced in ages and cost a great deal, as far as Ronan had heard.

Wasn't as if advanced university chemistry classes or guarding a supernatural detention center got a guy much in the way of off-market products knowledge.

"Black market gets us stuff that's never used anymore," Benjamin said as he hauled out an ancient-looking bag of cement mix. "We have a small supply from the trading post down the road. Scavengers find pockets of this stuff in abandoned buildings or buried at old sites and sell it for not much. It's worth nothing out in the real world."

"Real world."

Benjamin dusted a hand over the guard patch on the front of Ronan's uniform shirt. "You know."

Ronan wiped dust from his eyes. "*My* world consisted of a frozen prison and pissing my day away in a room where I could hardly stand. Is that what we're calling the real world, now?" Until he'd decided to trust Tatima. Just thinking her name made a sizzle deep in the center of himself.

Benjamin smiled in an eerie way that made Ronan's spine shiver. "The world we all thought we knew is long gone. Even if it still existed, it would be gone for you all the same. Now that you've run, you're a traitor."

"Aren't you also a traitor?"

Across from Ronan the man paused, smiling slightly. "Oh, sure. Our supposed fellow humans, this government of ours, they took the woman who brought me into this world. Said they knew what was causing her headaches, and then once they had her they said she couldn't come home because she'd been altered. We never saw her again. Fuckers don't deserve my loyalty."

Ronan dipped his head, wondering about his own mother—the drug that hastened her death was now used as a supernatural genocide weapon. About Tatima and how she'd been imprisoned. "Man. What's wrong with the world? I was an apathetic asshole at university, after my mother died. Fucked around, drank and got my brain twisted, but I never had the urge to screw over another person for no reason."

Ben shrugged. "I'm sure there are reasons. Power, fear, money. Preservation. People get crazy when all those things come into play."

Ronan shook his head. He rolled up his sleeves and put his attention toward grabbing bricks, and helping Benjamin. There were too many questions. And nobody Ronan trusted had answers.

Chapter Fifteen

Journal entry: 10.22.2668 (night)

I knew trouble would come, but I hoped we'd get farther before it caught us.

Tatima woke earlier, ate, and for a short while we both went back to sleep. We had a few really blissful moments together in a soft bed, just two bodies feeling the comfort of one another. But it was way too brief.

Darkness is falling now, and we need to move. I wanted to allow her to rest longer. Not possible. I hear a rhythmic, beating noise in the distance. Marching. Trucks.

It's time for us to race the enemy. Again.

Just hit me what I wrote down: I'm part of an "us" now, and the pure humans are the enemy. The other ones.

What does that make me?

***

Ronan shoved his journal in his pack and pushed at Tatima's shoulder, but her eyes had already opened. Her sleepy smile turned narrow and calculating in an instant. He found himself torn, both grateful and angry that she seemed to have already clued into what was coming. That fleeting peace on her face had relaxed him.

"Someone's coming?" Clearly, she already knew the answer to her own question and rose to a crouch in the center of the small bed.

"I think so. I hear engines and I smell smoke. I can't imagine anyone would be stupid enough to give away their position except a bunch of post guards storming through. We need to go. Fast."

The door to the small, stark bedroom opened with a slam that rattled the room's darkened windows. Charles ushered them out with a wave of his ropy arms. For a man the age Ronan's father would be, he kept in excellent shape. "Down to the cellar, you two. Out the far door,

99

there's a tunnel. It'll dump you farther into the words and away from the house."

Ronan shook his head, wondering why he hadn't thought to ask when they were doing the bricks earlier in the day. He'd assumed it was a utility closet and left it alone. With a word of thanks, they hurried to the cellar before making their getaway down a dirt-packed corridor.

Blood rushed heavy and loud between Ronan's ears when they came up from under a stone slab, only to find themselves facing a golden dance of flames through the trees.

He gripped Tatima's hand. "Run. Now."

"What— Oh, God." She stared in horror.

"Come on." He cut left, leading them through the trees, not in the way they'd planned to go and not back the way they'd come, but away from the road and their intended destination. Whoever was looking for them would be checking the roads. Perhaps this would confuse their pursuers.

They'd picked up speed when Tatima gasped and pulled up short, strangling the blood flow to his hand. The stricken look on her face stopped him from urging her forward. Then Ronan saw the horror.

Heads. On pikes. Bodies, both animal and human swinging from the petrified trees. Had they thought to scare her, or did they think the smell of blood would draw her out? Both?

Her hand trembled in his. "Ronan," she said. "I can see through the trees. They're all around us."

"Yes." He reached to his side for his firearm, counting shadows through the trees. Tough to tell what was movement and what was a dead body swinging in warning, but by his estimation he'd have enough charge time to take out a few of them, at most. "Try not to look."

Next to him, Tatima's breath sawed, heavy and ragged. "I think... There's only one solution."

"Yes." They'd have to fight their way through and hope they made it to the road. He stepped forward, gripping his weapon in both hands. "Okay. On my count we'll—"

Tatima released an unholy snarl. A fearsome, growling attack sound he'd never expect to come from a creature so beautiful. A creature whose mouth he'd had his lips on only hours before, when he'd kissed her before they lay down to sleep.

She sank into a crouch and regarded him with wide, glowing eyes that reflected the inferno through the trees. It looked as if she, herself, might catch fire. While Ronan tried to figure out what had caused her sudden change, a ball of flame shot through the trees, and she swiped at him with her claws extended.

Pain radiated through Ronan's body. He shouted from the surprise and pain when her nails scraped his neck and shoulder. The shock made him drop his duffel.

They both grabbed at the bag. With her superior speed, Tatima got it first. She launched into the air, springing toward a low tree. She propelled herself again over the heads of the shooters. Where she went after, Ronan couldn't know. His face met with the dirt courtesy of someone else's hand, his arm wrenched behind his back. Fighting through the scalding pain, he managed to flip and plant his feet, struggling against whoever held him down. He couldn't tell. They all wore masks.

A massive Sarkum cannon got shoved right in Ronan's face, and the battle more or less was lost. Those things could blow a fist-sized hole through steel. Then again, maybe it had been over when Tatima's thumbnail had clawed at his throat and she'd bounded through the trees like some fucking extinct monkey.

He'd never believed her capable of such a thing. She'd hidden it so well. What a fucking fool.

The burn of those nails digging into his skin lingered even as her presence faded—far less painful than the burn of her sudden betrayal, which left a hole larger than any man's fist.

In a fucked-up way, Ronan understood. She needed to save herself. Find her son. Still, she hadn't only left him behind, she'd left him wounded. Made it harder for him to fight or follow.

Why? He'd made love to her. Allowed himself to care.

He'd been so fucking wrong.

"Now, let's see what we've got." An arm came down in front of the cannon in Ronan's face, wrenched him by the short hairs on top of his head, and yanked backward so he had no choice but to stare up at the stars.

Which was good, really. Ronan hoped it kept the acrid taste of Tatima's betrayal from showing on his face. The burn and ache in his gut, the blood that flowed down his throat and collarbone... he wanted to hide everything. The blood would be impossible. She'd really taken a piece of him.

The rest? The rest he'd keep hidden inside his heart. He didn't want anybody to know how he'd let a parasite get close. Far too close.

Regardless, he'd be punished as a traitor. God knew how they would use it against him if they knew he'd shared his body and blood with her.

The man on the other end of the cannon in Ronan's face pulled down his black mask. "Nice try, Ronan. You really thought you'd get away?"

Jesus. "Kebro?" The one friend—he'd thought, anyway—he'd had in that place. The man was doing his job, but on the heels of Tatima leaving him the way she had, this tasted to Ronan like betrayal.

Kebro had never been a friend. Perhaps Tatima had never been that sweet girl she'd seemed back at his father's company. Or she'd changed and hidden it well. Either way, she'd used him.

Kebro grinned. "Yeah, I thought you started acting sketchy after they brought in that parasite bitch. The one the papers said killed your dad. You thought I didn't know why you wanted to be moved to the max ward?" He shook his head. "Stupid fucker." With a grin, Kebro brought back his fist. "Time to sleep, asshole."

***

Tatima ran.

Cold stung her and frozen tree branches sliced her skin as she swung from a broken branch and raced through the icy forest. Panic gripped her, blinding her eyes and weaving her steps.

Think, Tati. Think.

She stopped short and spun with a spray of dirt, heading for the house they'd come from. The men who helped before. They might not want to get involved. They probably wouldn't. Giving someone food and a space to sleep was far different from coming out of hiding for a rescue mission. Still, going back for Ronan alone would be suicide.

Suicide was her backup plan.

She brought a bloody hand to her face as she pummeled the door. Scraping Ronan had given her enough to smell, to taste, and, God willing, a trail to follow. Most likely they wouldn't have patched him up right away. The betrayal on his face when she'd scratched him made her heart ache, but that wound was necessary. Finding him was necessary.

"Get in here, girl." A strong arm snaked out the cracked door and pulled her inside the small house. The older one. Charles.

"I'm so sorry to come back here like this. They've got Ronan. We were outnumbered. It was either go with the guards or run, but I can't just let them take him." She threw a pleading look at the two men who had seemed so kind, now worrying at her with hardened faces. Perhaps she shouldn't have come.

Charles gave a nod toward the door. "Sounds like they brought the big guns out there."

"They did. I have to get Ronan. They'll kill him for helping me escape."

The younger one, Benjamin, pushed open a heavy panel under the staircase leading to the home's upper level. Guns, the kind that made the ones in Ronan's bag look like children's toys, came out. One old-looking weapon came off a shelf, something like the pistols she'd seen in museums when she was a child, but a glaring red in color.

"Flare gun. Take it," Chuck told her. "And these." A pile of cartridges landed in her hand. "Want you to step outside, fire three of 'em at the sky. Save the rest in case anybody comes at you. It's not the best for aiming, but it'll burn a hole in a man if they get close enough, and it's better than having to fight hand-to-hand. Now, let's go. We're right beside you."

Confused and jittery, Tatima did as instructed. She stepped outside and with shaking hands fired three shots into the night sky that echoed with a loud crack and a trail of red smoke. "Okay. What did I just do except alert the outpost guards to our presence?"

Charles laid a hand on her shoulder. "You called the cavalry. Now let's move."

They trekked swiftly, heading in the direction of the noise and smoke. Tatima stopped briefly to tease out all the smells, the blood and the fires and the oil from their groaning, grinding vehicles, to locate Ronan.

"This way."

"Tatima." She froze, aiming her small, useless-seeming flare gun.

A large shape stepped from behind the trees. "It's me, girl. It's Noah."

Her chest nearly collapsed from relief. "Why didn't you get word to me you were at the prison? I almost blew your cover when I saw you."

"I had a plan. When I realized Ronan was working on getting you out, I figured I'd let him take the lead. Back you up with transport. I could tell he was one of the good ones."

"Well, we've got a problem. The guards from the outpost caught up with us."

"I've got you covered. Let me head up and see what I can see." Noah slid into the shadows once more. An engine started and lights flashed as he pulled away, a sign she hoped, that he was going to do what he'd said.

She spun, dizzy from adrenaline. "What now?"

Charles answered by ratcheting his weapon. "Calm down, girl. We've got help coming."

Voices in the trees turned her around again. "Chuck. Got your message. What are we doing?"

"Got a friendly down. Guard from North Woods who released this young lady and set off a riot that busted the place wide-open."

A click and a buzzing noise told Tatima that Chuck's weapon was charging. Good. They'd need all the help they could get.

"What's the plan?" Someone from the back raised a hand.

"Tatima, you got your boy's scent?"

Her boy. Strangely, she liked the way that sounded. "Yes."

"Good. Okay, so we back her up. She's got the scent so let her lead, take out anything in the surrounding area that tries to stop us. After she's got him secure, we'll round up the rest of the guards. Easy enough?"

Murmurs of assent wrapped around Tatima, filling her chest with nervous gratitude. So many people had shown her the worst of humanity. These people knew what she was, and they were helping.

They were *helping*. She didn't have to do this alone.

"Thank you. All of you. Thank you so much."

It seemed not nearly enough to say.

"We're all in this, girl." A flash of lightning flew from Chuck's gun, hitting a stray guard who had come from the darkness. "Now. Looks like it's time to get a move on."

She drew a deep breath and plowed ahead, her mind focused on Ronan. His scent. A riot of sound and light exploded in the trees, shouts and cracks as the men around her cleared the way.

A harsh cry came from behind her as Charles, the man who'd selflessly come to her aid, went down. She turned to check him over, finding a deep wound in his shoulder.

"I'm so sorry. Let me help you. I can fix this."

He waved her on with his other arm. "Don't. Go on ahead. Save that young man."

"But..." She couldn't simply leave him. Not after all he'd done.

Another man, wearing a backpack and carrying some strange weapon Tatima hadn't seen, came out of the trees. He crouched low by Charles, looking him over. "I'll take it from here. Go."

So she turned back in the direction of the clearing she'd spotted ahead. The one where the smell of Ronan's blood rose far too cleanly over the fire, and the smell of burning flesh.

Finally, she found him. With that vile guard hovering above. Ronan looked.... Well, she didn't know how he was still alive.

A growl rose in her throat as she flew toward them.

Chapter Sixteen

Electricity arced from Ronan's hands to the soles of his feet. It was all he could do not to beg for the black, bliss of unconsciousness.

Kebro stood over him with a mild smile on his face and a control fob clutched in his fingers. With the squeeze of the asshole's hand, electricity bowed Ronan's body, his muscles and nerves at the mercy of a power far greater than his brain. They gave him enough juice to make him scream, enough to make him wish he was dying. Not enough to do him in for real.

The bastard seemed to calculate each jolt. Ronan would get no blissful return to blackness.

"Welcome back," Kebro murmured.

Ronan tried to keep still, but couldn't. The currents made his muscles twitch. "Thank you for the hospitality," he groaned. He resisted the temptation to flex his hands against the weights on them. They probably had him strung through with a powered tether. Ronan had seen them used in prisoner interrogations. It embedded into the hands, feet and testicles to send current through the entire body. Nasty stuff.

Nothing weighed on his balls at the moment, but fuck if he was going to feel around and check. No way would he give Kebro the satisfaction of showing either anxiety or clarity.

Kebro shook his head, still stooped over. "Didn't think you'd be the kind to turn against humanity, Ronan. Saw it comin' though. That parasite came in the door and you started acting all funny." Kebro straightened and smacked his lips thoughtfully. "At first I thought you were gonna snap her neck, or fuck her. Do whatever to work out your shit and call it a day." He leaned forward and flicked Ronan's forehead with a finger. "Then you got all distracted and shifty. Asking questions about shit you shouldn't. Jesus, helping a parasite escape? Your father's killer? That's fucked in the head."

A heavy smack shook Ronan's teeth. Anything. He'd offer Kebro anything now to close his eyes and let the void swallow him whole. Money, food, sex, the keys to the goddamned kingdom. Trouble was, he had nothing that Kebro would want. One look in the eyes of his former friend told Ronan he could only provide satisfaction with his misery.

He laughed and spat blood from his mouth. "You could say I was enlightened." Nothing he could say would bring Kebro down from his psychotic high. Might as well taunt the psycho.

"Oh yeah? Enlightened?" Another smack. Ronan's body jerked, bending and shuddering with another jolt. "Where'd that new enlightenment come from, friend? Parasite pussy?"

Metallic tastes and live sparks burst in Ronan's head when he ground his back teeth at the thought of what he'd shared with Tatima being cheapened. He flexed his fingers against the urge to hurl a fist at Kebro, knowing he'd hurt himself more than anything. "Yeah. Exactly right, my friend. The earth moved. The heavens opened."

Kebro's bloodied knuckles landed between Ronan's eyes with another blinding crack. He drew back and held up the controller. "You stupid *fuck*—"

Ronan screamed until his throat burned raw when the charge fired. He swore his body boiled from the inside out. His pulse shot into what was left of the stratosphere as he gasped for breath. "Look, she had answers. She'd been an employee of my father's... If I earned her trust..." Ronan panted through the pain. "She knew about my father's death. I just...wanted..." He struggled to think. Maybe if he gave them enough of the truth, Kebro would cease the torture. Maybe nothing mattered.

Through the fog of agony, Ronan's anger slipped through his fingers. He really did understand why she'd gone. Her child had to be saved.

Still, Ronan couldn't help but think that with her strength and his weapons, they could have fought their way out if she'd stayed. His chest burned as he let his body sag, too weighed down by the pain and the frustration of it all.

Goddammit, he'd given her a piece of himself. Why did remembering that now make his eyes burn?

It's only the pain. You can use that. Focus on the pain.

"Of course she knew about your father's death," said Kebro. "*She killed him.* You coulda questioned her back at North Woods, dumbass. We got interrogation rooms."

Through swollen eyes, Ronan scanned the perimeter. A bonfire burned, illuminating some of the heads on pikes that still lingered in the woods, preserved well thanks to the winter air. "Did you kill all of these men?"

"Not men." Kebro spread his arms wide. "Creatures. Those fucking supernaturals all tried to make a mass exodus when you pulled your escape stunt in the minimum-security wing." A strange mix of hate and curiosity laced Kebro's voice. He bent close to Ronan's face. "You know, I get it. I was into one once. Even thought I loved her. A heila-hybrid." He sneered. "Came out of a lab in New Texas with wide eyes and a sexy drawl that made her seem sweet and innocent, like a baby animal. Boy, she had the body of an angel and a mouth that made you wanna do bad, bad things. When the uprising happened and the states got separated my friend, you bet your ass she turned and took sides. They all did. *The supernaturals cannot be trusted.*"

Kebro launched spit into Ronan's face. With the blood on his skin and the freezing temperatures out in the woods, Ronan hardly felt the wetness. If this torture shit didn't do him in before he figured something out, the weather sure would. Tatima had taken his coat, and it was getting awfully fucking cold.

Ronan struggled now against the thin wire cords that held him, numb enough to ignore the pain. "I'm not convinced humans can, either." Hurt and anger burned bright. He hated Tatima for leaving, even though she should have. But someone at his father's company stood to gain from his father's death, and Ronan still wondered if she'd been involved—or had she given him the truth?

Kebro stepped back, holding the red-buttoned fob high in the air. He smiled tightly. "That's for fucking sure. I thought we might have been buddies. Turns out you were only stepping on me to get someplace better." He pressed another button. "Well, you'll learn what that buys, friend."

Ronan tensed, waiting for the electric slam of pain. Instead, he heard a zipping sound in the trees. The cords jerked tight around his body. This time he clamped his mouth tight, determined not to scream as the wires tugged his body upward. "Fucking bastard." He barely whispered the words, but Kebro heard.

"You're the one who broke the rules."

"Where is everyone else?" Agony made Ronan choke on his question. Most likely pain would knock him unconscious again, and then the wires would cut through his skin until he bled out. He prayed it would happen fast.

"Wilkes and Drivens will return shortly to help me take your body down and present you to the commander. We have a team tracking down your girl. Everybody else is putting out fires at the outpost, thanks to your bullshit." He cocked an eyebrow. "Managed to do some real damage, between you and those other prisoners who got out after. Nice one."

It almost sounded like a real compliment.

Ronan didn't answer. He tried to accept the sensation of the wires clawing into his skin, but relaxing his body put the force of his weight against the thin metal. Tensing himself would only tire him faster. His heart hammered and he thought rapid fire of Tatima and then of his parents, alternately certain the best solution was to fight, or to give in and die.

Then, he heard noises. Wild, bloodcurdling screams.

Wet splatters. Thumps. Ripping.

Kebro turned, and the smug smile slid from his face. A taloned hand gripped his throat from behind. When he fell, a wrathful Tatima with wild hair and glowing eyes stood in his place.

Ronan struggled against the wires, but Tatima's arm reached out, gripping him as if he weighed nothing.

"Stop," she said. "Let me cut you down."

"What...?" He gasped, trying to get control of himself through the fog. "I thought you fled."

"That might have been smarter," she said. "But we're kind of a team." She indicated the sounds coming through the petrified forest. "I'm sorry for disappearing. I went back to get Charles and Benjamin. They rounded up a few friends. I thought it would be safer with help." Triumph glowed on her face when she held up a now blood-covered controller and pushed—thank God—the right button to lower him to the ground.

"I couldn't tell you," she whispered. "They'd have heard me and known where to follow."

Body aches pummeled Ronan. He grunted when his back hit the dirt. Standing was a real challenge when his legs wouldn't hold him up.

"But you attacked me."

"I scratched you so I could track you. And so maybe they'd think we weren't working together. Too much to hope I see, but it seemed like a good plan at the time."

"Don't struggle." Tatima brushed her lips over his before getting to work on untangling the wires that held him.

"You healed my body and got me out of that prison, Ronan. Now it's my turn to help you."

Chapter Seventeen

Entry: 10.24.2668 (Tatima)

You've been unconscious since I cut you down from that tree. I'm sorry for what I had to do. If you live, I hope you understand my reasons. I hope you accept my apology.

I don't know if you'll trust me again. I think we've both been trying our best in the middle of a world that does not reward trust. I did what I had to, so that we could both survive.

When this is over, I'm hoping we have a chance. Is that crazy, the thought of you and me having a future? Or is it crazy to hope we'll even make it to tomorrow?

—T

***

Dark surrounded him. Ronan thrashed against the arms that held him. "Let me the fuck go, Kebro, you piece of shit—"

"Hey, Tati. He's awake." The low, smooth words did not come from Kebro.

Then Ronan remembered Kebro was dead. He struggled again, this time to get his bearings. They were someplace dark, and his head pounded like a gang of outpost guards had used it for tactical practice. He couldn't get himself upright. "What the fuck is going on?" He was draped over someone's shoulders. "Put me the fuck down." He tucked and tried to roll out of the iron arms that held him in place.

"Tati, he's struggling. Don't want him to hurt himself none."

Warm fingers touched his face. "Ronan, it's okay. You're with friends."

"Friends?" He shifted side to side, testing the grip of whoever had him. "A friend would put me down."

"You lost a great deal of blood and you kept fighting. We were afraid you'd reopen a wound. Anyway, you couldn't walk on your own." She ran her hands over his hair, across his back, his arms, which he realized then were bare.

Tatima's touch slowed the crazed rush of Ronan's breath and blood. The fact that leaning into her hand felt as natural as his own skin gave him real pause. Sweat broke out on his chilled back. "Where are my clothes?"

"You've still got your pants." Amusement sounded in her voice. "We had to get rid of your shirt. I ripped it apart to stem all the places you were leaking blood. I think I saw another in your pack." Her lips brushed his ear when she leaned close to his head. "Noah will put you down if you promise to be still, okay? I went through a lot to get you healed and I'd like you to stay that way."

"Noah?" When Ronan settled on his feet, he wondered if his equilibrium had taken a holiday. He managed to right himself with some help from a nearby wall, but his head buzzed as if he still had one of those wires in him.

They were inside a building so cold it made the North Woods Outpost seem cozy. The darkness prevented much looking around.

As he felt around, he realized everything from the wall to a cloth-covered table had a soft texture against his skin. He rested his forehead against the inviting surface, marveling. Walls hardly got painted like this anymore. "Where are we?"

"Inside the old Imperial Hotel." Noah came closer. Ronan could tell from the volume of the voice and the footsteps, and his vision slowly adjusted to make out shadows. "Lower ball room," the man continued. "It's under private ownership now. Can't get in here if you don't have an entry code, so it's safe for us to lay low."

"We're in Boston?" Ronan looked around even though he couldn't see. Without thought he reached out, needing to touch Tatima. He tried to convince himself he only wanted to know where she was, that holding her didn't help him breathe. "How did we make it here? Where are my things? Why can't I fucking see?" It should be good that they'd made it this far, but having missed the trip turned his brain.

Across from Ronan, Noah chuckled. "We are indeed, or what remains. Right across the fucking street from your target, thank you very much. This hotel is closed to the public now but in its heyday, we were living large. Even after the rebellion, we made money for a long while, hiding the supes and helping them out of the city." He turned then. "Come on, let's make tracks. I need to do a perimeter check, and I want to see you to the tunnel."

"Thank you for doing this," Tatima said as she pulled Ronan's hand.

He stiffened, hating the position he'd landed in only slightly less than the one he'd found himself in with Kebro and those fucking electrical wires. He was reliant on Tatima to lead him through an inky blackness so dark his eyes could have been closed, and a man he still didn't know well was the one helping them to supposed safety. Still, rudeness would get him nowhere. "Yes. Thank you," he said.

"Our kind has led the underground movement since the beginning," Noah said. "Gotta turn this shit into something good."

Our kind?

"And with this new assbag running for office, the safety of all our brothers and sisters is more critical than ever. None of us can afford to sit by and watch."

Tatima said something that whistled through Ronan's ear like smoke, because right then his night vision finally kicked in with a holy fucking *no way*. He'd never been able to see in the dark like this before. "Oh my God..."

It was like someone had handed him night goggles. The supercharged kind he remembered from his training...the kind that the snipers used. He must have stopped because the two figures walking in front of him did too. Tatima, bathed in a golden glow.

"Noah, that's really you?" He couldn't believe he'd heard right.

Noah huffed a breath. "Hey, friend."

Ronan scowled. "I can't believe you got out. I left you— Kebro made it sound like—You're not human? How did you pass the DNA screening before guard duty?"

Noah wiggled his eyebrows. "I got the extra special DNA. I'm a Subject A."

Ronan stopped. Rumors of a limited small-group study had flitted around his father's lab, but they'd been dismissed as urban legend. Thought to be able to mimic another's body completely, the few known test subjects from a lab in Delaware known as Subject A had all disappeared. "The literature says you all died. Intolerance to the lab conditions."

A low chuckle from Noah. "Oh, sure. We know literature never lies." He pushed one fist into the palm of his hand. "We hide ourselves well, man. Intolerance my dark ass. It's a big danger that we can pass for human. Also makes us tough as hell for them to find."

"Right. Still. Shit." Noah put himself at one mother fucker of a risk at the outpost, even if he could pass. He hadn't been subtle about his opinions.

"Hey, friend. No risk, no reward."

The golden glow around Noah's broad face and body got stronger, the contrast higher, the farther they got along the stairwell they descended. It made no sense as they were moving from a floor with no windows to an even deeper basement with what smelled like mold in its depths.

Ronan reached for Tatima's shoulder again. "All of a sudden, my vision's all crazy. I can see everything." And...he inhaled deeply. "Smell everything. I smell blood." His pulse picked up. An odd sort of arousal filled him when he realized what he smelled. Not fear, not concern, but excitement? *This is want.*

He licked his lips.

Ahead of him, Tatima's steps faltered. "We had to bring your friend Kebro with us so his absence wouldn't be missed so fast. I fed from his body so I could heal. You're smelling the remnants left behind."

Ronan swallowed, suddenly thirsty. He longed for water so desperately his tongue throbbed. Water or... he stopped walking again. What was that aftertaste in his mouth? "You—"

Before Ronan could speak, Noah turned. "This is where I take my leave. You're welcome to use the staff quarters if you need to rest before you head out. If I don't see you beforehand, be well."

When he'd departed, Ronan turned to Tatima. "You fed me your blood, right? I can taste that coppery flavor." He ran his hands all over his body. "I should have realized. My wounds..."

Was that why he smelled blood? Why he was thirsty? Would he turn into one of them now? What would happen to him? He didn't know what could come from this. He'd read of dangerous consequences. There was always the chance that not everything he'd been told in training was shit.

He gripped her arm with a shaky hand. "Tatima, I told you not to do this."

Chapter Eighteen

Tatima tried to be casual while she loaded things into a bag. She'd assured him her blood was safe, but the chill he emitted from across the room proved he didn't quite trust her.

Ronan cleared his throat, fingering the ripped edges of a book in his hand. His journal. "Did you pull pages out of this?"

Nerves gripped her belly. "You said writing helped you think. I decided to try." Her breath whooshed out, shy of the "I'm sorry" perched on her lips. She'd clearly upset him, but she would not apologize. They were no longer in that prison, and she'd done what was necessary to save him. No. She refused to apologize.

"You also left me a message in here."

"I wasn't sure there would be time to talk."

His face reddened. "The things I wrote in here were personal."

"I didn't read what you wrote." She sat on the bed she'd been using to organize her things. The beat of her heart hammered out confusion. They'd gone from enemies to lovers in such a short while. "And everything we've been through together is personal." After all, even as enemies hadn't it still been personal? They'd still had history, of a sort.

Were they back to enemies because she'd given him her blood?

Body tight and hot, Tatima strode forward. "I saved your life, Ronan. It was the only way. Had I not given you my blood, you and I wouldn't be talking now. And you're angry? How about a thank you?"

He huffed a breath. "I know. You're right. There are things—a man doesn't always like to share his fears. The things they told us in training... A lot of those things were wrong, but I don't want to assume."

She tried to rub the exhaustion from her eyes. "Ronan, I'm sorry, but I swear you're fine. Do you know what I found out about why those experiments were held? You worked in that lab, you should have some idea. Aside from being jerks until someone gets the urge to kill them, humans basically die because they rust to death. Oxygen, the thing we must breathe to survive, it corrodes your insides. *My DNA, my blood,* was altered in a lab to be the antidote to that corrosion."

She nudged forward, into his space, her chest against his. He didn't push away. "If the side effects of altering us hadn't been so awful, it actually might have been a pretty neat upgrade."

Ronan sighed, pressing his forehead against hers. "I guess craving blood and never seeing daylight is a hell of a side effect."

"The sensitive sense of smell is no good either, in my opinion. I don't need to know when someone a quarter of a mile away made soy loaf for dinner, you know?"

Ronan poked her in the side. She was trying to lighten his mood, and they needed all the light they could get at the moment. "You did what you did to help me. I *do* thank you for that. In spite of my helping you escape, I find it's hard to let go of all the training."

She pushed herself away from him with the slap of her hand on the wall. "It isn't simply training though, right? It's me. The effects of the blood will wear off, Ronan, I swear. Sooner than you might like. At least, those were the testing results. 'Subjects benefits do not outweigh the potential negative effects,' they said. What they meant was that the benefits like the increased healing and strength went away too quickly. I heard the staff say there were addiction problems in the field. Best to keep people afraid of touching us than become dependent."

"Addiction?"

"Only if you keep drinking more and more to prevent the effects from wearing off. Once is safe. You don't have to worry."

"No, I'm not..." He reached forward to grab hold of her clothing. To pull her forward again. To brush the softness of her cheek with his hand. "Okay. I'm sorry. You're right that I bought the party line. It was stupid, but I was pissed off with a one-track mind. You're also right that I still held concern about what you and your blood might do to me. I'm not a lab tech anymore, Tatima. I don't study this stuff. But...I didn't mean to insult you."

Ronan took a deep breath and tugged gently, willing Tatima forward. Slowly, step by step, she came forward.

Finally, she brushed her nose against his. "We're both starting over again when it comes to trusting and understanding each other. We'll work it out." She'd had long nights of solitary thinking to get used to what she knew about herself. It had to be hard for him.

He brushed his hand down her back. "You know this thing might be suicide. What we're about to try."

Her heart lurched. "I know. But you know I still have to try. You want answers from Fairfield." Tears welled in her eyes. "And he has my baby."

When he put his arms around her, she wished for a blink that they could simply fall into the bed and stay there until everything bad outside disappeared. Being wrapped in his arms, she'd managed to forget for a minute.

"I think we need a better plan," he said. "If we manage to make it inside, I don't think we should split up once you find Valo."

She cast a glance in his direction. "What are you going to do, go with us all the way to the western border?" Flutters kicked up in her stomach again.

Stay. She did want him to go with them, but it was way too much to ask.

"Might as well. I can't return home, or to North Woods." Ronan gave a final nod. "Wouldn't go back there even if I had the option."

"Right. That makes sense. Of course." Tatima eased away, returning to the supplies she'd been packing. Things she wanted to say but shouldn't burn in her throat, making it sore.

"Tatima"

The low tone he used to speak her name hit her in the belly. Maybe he *did* want to go to the border with her for more than only safety reasons.

"I'm glad you came back to get me out of those woods."

Oh. That dull ache slid down to her toes. "I wouldn't have left you there to be killed."

"You could have. You probably should have."

She turned, and he was so close that their noses brushed. "Not after what you did for me," she whispered.

"Well." His cool hands wrapped around her upper arms. "Again, you have my thanks. What about Noah? I don't understand how he got away from the station without being detected."

"He can mirror any human with whom he's had physical contact. All he had to do was become somebody who had the authority to leave without being questioned. They tested him at your father's lab for a brief period of time. What he can do is pretty amazing."

Ronan's mouth dropped open. "The day I was in the commander's office, Noah was outside waiting." He rubbed at the back of his neck. The wrinkle of his forehead suggested he was still trying to figure it all out. "The commander... Nice trick," he murmured.

Tatima smiled sadly and backed away. She pulled a shirt out of his bag and handed it over. "Here, your skin feels cold. Put this on. I think you're healed enough to dress." She looked him up and down. His skin glowed and his muscles flexed with every move of his body. Honestly, he looked amazing. "Your wounds have all closed. Even so, you were unconscious all day today, and you need to regain strength. Shivering will only expend useless energy."

Ronan's focus wandered off into deep thought. "I don't recall it being hard to get into my father's building. Then again, it sounds as if a great deal has changed in my absence." Back to her. "We should go now, rather than wait. Why leave your son any longer than necessary?"

She squeezed his hand. "Believe me, I want to go now. I want to go last week. You *know* we have to be careful. It may be taller and shinier on the outside, but inside, that place wasn't much better than North Woods Outpost. Hasn't been since your father retired..." She stepped back, choking on a sob. "I'm sorry. I didn't want to have to say something like that to you. Your father, he didn't know. When he came back to visit, he would talk to my son and give him cookies. He didn't seem to see all the things Fairfield had gotten into." She wrapped her arms around herself. "He gave up too much. Aside from stopping in to look around once in a while, he had no control. He should have."

Her own whispered accusation chilled her. Would Ronan hate her all over again for blaming his father about the way Fairfield had abused his power?

Her heart slowed...skipped...nearly stopped while she waited for Ronan to return her jab with a slap in the face, real or otherwise.

"Tatima, I'm sorry." He moved toward her slowly, shoulder rolling. Hands in his pockets. He still hadn't put on a shirt, and it made the expanse of his chest look that much more inviting when he held out his arms. "I'm so sorry."

"It's... I only wanted you to understand." Warmth and moisture slipped down her cheeks, in spite of her protests. Nobody had ever told her they were sorry for her pain. She'd swear she didn't need anybody's sympathy, but Ronan's touched her and warmed her inside.

"I'm so sorry," he said again, his breath hot in her ear this time. Strong arms folded around her. "I wish I could have been there to protect you."

"Don't." Tatima took the deepest breath she could, filling her lungs and standing tall, even in the safe and comforting warmth of his arms. She stayed close but took one step, needing to breathe. "We can't change what's in the past. We're alive, that's what matters. And I don't want you to be sorry," she said. "I want to make them pay."

Chapter Nineteen

Journal entry: 10.24.2009 (almost midnight)

She said it was Fairfield's mistress who attacked Dad. Fairfield's mistress, who'd been turned blood-sucker from the same batch of test subjects as Tatima. I don't understand why a guy who's been so vocally anti-supernatural would have a genetically altered mistress. Or why he'd even be running those experiments at all. Did something change his mind? The way my mind changed about Tatima, only in reverse? Was this woman simply disposable to Fairfield?

Lucky for us, the moon is a speck tonight. That piece that broke off 'round about a hundred years ago is one of the reasons for the limited water supply now, or so the weather guys speculate. Sucks for practical reasons, but it's gonna work in our favor now. No light will make getting into Dad's building easy.

I decided I'm not gonna worry about questioning Fairfield. No. Worry is the wrong word. I'll worry, I suppose, but what Tatima needs is what matters. A little boy has been without his mother. Maybe sick, probably scared. God knows what else.

I'm done with the idea of revenge. Look where it almost got me with Tatima.

I think about how angry I was at the start of my assignment at North Woods, and now what I want is to see a kid reunited with his mother. Too many things have gone from bad to the fifth world war over misunderstandings. It's time I focused on doing good. If I can make Fairfield taste his own medicine, that's a bonus.

***

Ronan took inventory of his things. He checked his weapon, and they split the vials of Ellanol in case they could come in handy. Anything they could carry went in a pocket for easy access. The rest was left behind in a room of the hotel servant's quarters. They tried to leave only the things that didn't matter, in case they didn't return.

To be extra safe, they decided to wait until the darkest hour of night. To ensure that any creatures in need of rescue from the building were most likely to be awake, but also to make sure that most of the humans were likely to be gone.

"I think this's everything." She zipped the duffel and dropped it at the foot of the bed, still covered in dust but soft sheets. It must have been a very nice hotel if even the employees slept on good bedding.

He ran his hand across the dusty comforter. "I bet this used to be a great place. I wonder how Noah's family had so much money."

She sat on the foot of the mattress. "Old money. Good investments. Then later, they helped supernaturals and ran supplies for the underground. Lucky thing." She sniffed. "Noah got enrolled in a study due to some rare blood condition, as I understand. His situation was different. The family used all their resources to get him free when the round-ups happened. It's so sad about his sister, though." A deep frown creased her forehead.

Ronan swallowed and nodded his head. They had longer to wait and nothing to say, both nervous about what they'd find across the street. Given what Tatima had told him about the testing she'd been subjected to, the hollow dread inside told Ronan her son was dead. Regardless of what he thought or feared, he wouldn't say so aloud. He'd spent unnecessary time checking and rechecking supplies so he didn't have to think.

"Makes sense."

Brilliant fucking response, Ronan.

A hiccupy sob came from her throat. Then another, louder. "Ronan, I'm scared. What if..."

"Hey. Hey, we'll get through this. Don't cry." *Please.* If she cried, Ronan wouldn't know what to do. He brought one hand to either side of her face, running his hands through her hair. Their hearts thumped against each other's. Ronan put his forehead to hers and breathed her in.

"It'll be fine. I'm sure he's fine." *Lies and more lies, Ronan.* He kissed her forehead and then her cheek. The only thing he wanted was to calm her trembling.

Really, Ronan? Is that all you want?

"We have to think positive." Sure, they could wish it all better. While he was wishing, Ronan would put them far away from all this shit, on a warm beach, making love.

As if she heard his inner thoughts, she brought her lips to his. "Thank you for all you've done."

He let his fingers tighten in her hair, her warmth linger against his for only a moment, before he pulled away. "No..." God help him, he did want her. But not like this. Not now.

She rose onto her knees. "You said we should wait a little longer. Until it was almost pitch dark outside. Is that wrong?"

He shook his head. "No, that's what I said."

The sweetness of her breath filled his senses. "You've forgiven me for healing you?"

"Yes." Ronan struggled to manage his breath. "That's sort of a shitty thing to hold a grudge about, when I think about it."

"You know..." She slid her fingers between his. "Your blood is inside me. Mine is in you. It's maybe the one good thing about this. It's a like we're connected, you know?"

He wasn't sure, but he sure as hell could swear he sensed all the things inside her. The blue of her eyes, cast gold with his temporary night vision, swirled with emotion.

"Tatima..." Ronan gritted his teeth. It felt wrong to want her when the world was about to come crashing down around them, but the blood in him—every nerve in his body—was dying for her. "God, I want—I don't know if we'll—" *We may never see each other again.*

"Ronan, I know. I know there's a chance we might not find Valo. We might not survive the night or even get inside the building. I know—" She shook her head, and sniffled. Her lip trembled. "It was good, before. Let me have that with you, while I know I still can."

His forehead fell against hers, her breath shallow, shaky, and sweet against his lips. When hers brushed against his, he kissed back. Her skin against his woke him up, and he needed this, too.

One last time.

He'd never been alive. Not this way. Not until Tatima. This could be the last night either of them would be.

"You're sure it's safe?" he said. He'd asked before, but he wanted to be certain. Now, while he was still thinking, at least a little.

You're thinking about safety now? In an hour you'll be storming your father's office. You don't know what's going to happen.

"I'm sure. I can't..." She made a sniffling sound. "My immune system is excellent. Thanks to all the experiments, I'm not fertile anymore."

He wrapped his arms around her as tight as he could manage. "Dammit, I'm sorry." He wanted to keep his arms around her forever.

"Stop. You can't keep apologizing. It wasn't you."

"Tatima, I was your fucking jailer." The fact burned in his stomach.

She palmed the back of his neck and pulled him against her. He savored the soft, fullness of her lips in that slow kiss. "And in the end, you were my rescuer," she whispered. "You saved me."

He closed his eyes and said a quick prayer, while he still had one last shred of self-control. "Maybe we saved each other." He ran his fingertips up her arm, feeling the energy inside him. More than he'd had before. No rage, nothing to dull with drink or with suspect club drugs. Only Tatima and her lips on his.

Even if it was only for that moment, Ronan Dempsey wasn't dying anymore. Thanks to Tatima, life coursed through his veins. "You're sure?"

Her lips brushed his. "Right now it's the only thing I'm sure of."

Ronan closed his eyes against the truth of her words.

They tasted each other slowly as he backed toward a bed. Ronan let her climb on top of him. He wanted her to be the one in control. A funny thing, since he'd always taken the lead in sex with other women. With Tatima, knowing what she'd been through, it felt right to hand over the reins.

They divested each other of pants and shoes, and he slid his fingers over each scar on her spine, wishing so many things had been different. Wishing *he* had been different.

"Ronan..." She hugged his hips with her thighs, and they both ascended to heaven one last time before they both made their foray into hell.

He clasped her hands, letting her press his knuckles to the mattress. As before, he wanted Tatima to set the pace. Doing so was different, thrilling in a way that made his heart spin in circles. At that moment he couldn't remember another woman who had come before, but he was sure he hadn't been a thoughtful lover. All he wanted now was for her to feel satisfied. To feel *safe*.

Tatima's warmth surrounded Ronan, and he clenched every muscle in his body with the desperate need for release. She rode him steadily, gripping him. Wringing pleasure from him with each stroke of her body.

Their whispers for more, to touch there, and gasps for breath filled the quiet room. Their stares met in the dark. Her glowing eyes held him captive.

With his vision sharpened by the infusion of Tatima's blood, Ronan could see things in her gaze that ought to frighten him. Passion and emotion swirled in the depths of her eyes. Ronan only wished he had his hands free so he could pull her close and let her know he wanted her the same way.

Promises lingered unspoken on his lips. He could hardly assure her of tomorrow, much less of what would happen after that. Still, a fierce insistence filled him to desperately shout out things he shouldn't with each frantic thrust.

Her hands clasped his. He arched upward as she undulated above him, matching him stroke for stroke.

"Tatima... I... didn't expect this." Fuck it, they had already been through hell together and they were about to willingly seek out more trouble. After everything, no way could he just let her go without telling her how he really felt. "I want... more. I need you," he whispered.

As he said that last part, Tatima's legs squeezed around him. Her head went back, fangs bared, with a cry of release.

The squeeze of her muscles and the sight of her body moving, the slick of her sweat-dampened skin under her fingers, pushed him over the edge. He grunted, taking advantage of the fact that she'd let go of his hands to pull her close.

Ronan tried to collect his thoughts. Tatima didn't respond to what he'd said. Maybe she hadn't understood. Or she hadn't heard the last part, uttered quietly before her orgasm.

Still, given her sensitive hearing and the way she avoided his eyes as she rose to dress, Ronan suspected she had.

He rubbed the sore spot on his chest and quietly rose to put on his clothes as they both got ready for what lay ahead.

Chapter Twenty

Journal entry:10.25.2668 (12:05 am)
I guess we're about to see what we're capable of, Tatima and I.
Here we go. God help us.

***

The still night chilled Ronan. Stillness gave the false illusion of calm. They hit the street from a tunnel that connected to the Old United sewer systems from the back of the Imperial Hotel, then crossed to the rear door of Dempsey Medical, aided by the fact that the night had reached its blackest point and what remained of the moon had waned.

As Ronan finished replacing the sewer cover, Tatima's hand landed on his shoulder. "There's something I almost forgot," she whispered.

He stopped. Suddenly stiff, he stood slowly. "The sound of your voice worries me."

"The door locks. After hours they require biometric validation for entry."

He took a few slow breaths before he turned to face her. "You didn't tell me because..." Frustration rose from the top of his head into the chilly night, like steam.

"I'm telling you now." Her refusal to meet his eyes and the lift of her chin told him she knew exactly why he was angry.

"Was this the reason you needed me on your side?" He didn't want to believe such a thing. The old habit of mistrust died hard. The idea of having been duped so completely made Ronan want to turn on his heel right then and walk away.

He was falling for her, for the love of God.

She snarled through her fangs. "Do we have to keep going in circles like this? We had so much to confront even getting out of that prison. I figured I'd handle the lock when it came time. I just wanted to find my

128

baby. You can come. You can stay if you don't trust me. I'm grateful to you for helping me, but I'm not going to stand here and allow you to question me *anymore*." She turned and headed for the back door.

He pushed past her. When they reached the security panel, he laid his finger against the coded device, wincing only for a moment as it bit his finger for a sample of his blood, and the indicator blinked to alert them they'd been cleared. "Lucky I'm still in the system. They had those locks on the biohazard lab when I was here before. What were you going to do if I hadn't come with you?"

She shrugged. "Use my strength to blast through one of the lobby windows. Try to short-circuit the security system. I wasn't sure." She sighed. "You're right. I told you, I wasn't even sure we'd get this far. I didn't know how to bring up the locks without you thinking exactly what you thought. I sort of hoped you'd know, but then you never mentioned anything about them in our planning. I'm sorry I didn't tell you. Clearly, it went over well."

Ronan shook his head. He couldn't blame her for her concerns. In the dim light of the foyer, with the building's canned air whipping at her hair and her uncertain face, her tired smile made him ache.

His slight soreness from their lovemaking made him curl his lips as they went for the stairs. "Well, we're here. I hope you'll trust me and be honest next time." *I hope there will be a next time.* "Now, come on. Whatever happens, we'll work it out. It's going to be okay."

A deep shuddering took hold of the building. Famous last words.

Tatima gripped the staircase. "Oh my God, what's happening? Valo!"

He grabbed her hand. "Where would he be?"

"Probably in the lab. I hope."

Fifth floor. They needed to hurry.

"Let's go." Once again, they ran. Goddamn, he hoped they could make it to a time and place where they didn't have to sprint for their damn lives.

When they emerged from the fifth-floor stairwell, they found the door unlocked and open. Fairfield stood waiting for them. Tall and bespectacled with graying hair, he sat at the receptionist's desk with his feet up. Smug fucking son of a bitch.

Ronan drew his firearm.

"The North Woods commander called me with word of your little rebellion. We've been keeping watch for you. It's lovely to see you again, Ronan, but I'd lower your weapon if the parasite wants her child in one piece."

Tatima's fingers dug into Ronan's shoulders, but he kept his focus trained on Fairfield.

"Don't listen to him," Ronan said. "For all we know, Valo isn't even here. A man who's willing to kill to take over someone's company is willing to do anything."

Fairfield smiled. "Ah, but that was my erstwhile mistress, seeking to avoid what was coming to her. I didn't do anything to harm your father."

Tatima charged forward. "Don't lie. Don't you *dare* lie. You were finished with her and you threw her away! It was you she went after, not Mr. Dempsey. She only wanted to stay alive!"

Tears ran down Tatima's face. Ronan's arms encircled her waist and pulled her back to his chest. He kept one arm around her while his shooting hand held his firearm steady. "Can't say I fault the lady's logic, sir."

Fairfield laughed. "Lady? Logic? Terrible misnomers." He sniffed like he'd smelled something rotten. "I can see she's lured you in with her charm. I once fell for a pretty face with fangs also, young man, but once they've been changed, they aren't the same as you and me. Guaranteed the shine will wear off that apple. When it does, the experience will be bitter."

Ronan pushed Tatima behind him, advancing. "Thanks, friend. I'll worry about my own apples. Tell us where her child is, or you're fucking dead."

"You would shoot the next president of the Eastern States?"

This joke of a human *was* the same Fairfield running for president? And somehow, he still thought he had a shot? Ronan squared his aim. Fuck this nut job.

"The election's over. You lost."

"Ah, no. You wouldn't have heard, being all the way up in those woods." Fairfield shook his head like there was honestly terrible news. "They're re-tallying the votes, which I am certain will come out in my favor. Lucky, as my opponent has gone missing. Presumed dead."

"He has a guard detail." This man was a cheating ladder climber. He'd broken fuck knew how many laws. God knew what else. Determination tightened Ronan's fingers around the grip of the gun. He leveled a glare over the muzzle at this man who'd probably killed his father before he'd turned his company into something dark and corrupt.

Hate bubbled up all over again. Fresh and hot.

Fairfield shrugged. "You'd think." He tsked. "Such a shame."

Around them the building quaked again, and yet Fairfield stood there, chatting with them like they were having a casual lunch. Something was wrong. He was—what—stalling?

Ronan took a step back, murmuring to Tatima low enough that the rumble would mask his voice, but loud enough she'd still hear him. "You know where you need to look?"

She nodded.

"I'll hold him. Go." Ronan charged, and when Fairfield glanced sideways, he knew they had a bigger problem. He considered the possibility that Fairfield had a guard of his own lurking somewhere. He fired anyway.

Fairfield screamed as the sizzle of Ronan's chemical bullet fragmented and plowed through his body. Fucking awesome. Even if the man wore a vest, these could worm their way through. "You little piece of shit—"

"Careful, sir, the more you move, the more the pieces migrate through your body. I'd try not to get overly excited." He raised his arm to fire again.

From the far end of the hall, Tatima screamed.

***

The lab Tatima remembered had changed. Fewer tables, microscopes, and little machines that spun test tubes.

More cages.

So. Many. Cages.

Hot and cold shot through Tatima's body in one jarring shot. This was worse, far worse, than even she had pictured.

She'd been kept in an enclosed unit, yes, but she'd been fed and cared for. The creatures in these cages... They did not look well.

Some were hybrids stuck in mid-change, or blood-suckers with damaged fangs. A thing she didn't recognize with scales and a half-broken wing.

These were the mistakes. The ones that were too damaged to simply ship off to a detention camp. Her heart broke.

"Valo!"

Her son lay in an open cage. Bloody. She pulled him into her arms and cradled him carefully, but her mind was spinning. She'd tried so hard to be strong, but right now she couldn't think past the sight of her child, looking so small and damaged.

Unconscious.

He needed help. So did these other creatures. She hugged her son to her chest, flipping the locks on cages while she went around the room. A young man coughed smoke and groaned as he eased out, but it was clear his right arm didn't work.

Her gaze swept the room. "This isn't going to work." Most of them couldn't get out on their own, and Tatima couldn't do anything for them while holding Valo.

She needed help. She needed Ronan.

***

Ronan ran down the hall, into a room so bright his eyes burned. The building shook more now, and falling equipment shattered on the floor.

Ronan found Tatima huddled by an open cell. The boy cradled in her arms lay pale and ashen, bleeding from recent slash marks to his arms.

"They knew." The words trembled out of her. "They knew we were coming. How?"

Ronan's throat burned. It had probably been a likely guess, once they made their escape. No need to upset her by saying so.

"It'll be okay. Let's get him out. We'll find a solution." He leaned to kiss her, but when he did, he picked up a sound that made him a liar. A boom of a door and retreating footsteps, more than one person. Ronan scanned the wreckage in the lab, the other clear doors behind which subjects had recently been bloodied and tortured.

"Fuck. Fairfield did have a guard. He probably brought someone to destroy evidence and we interrupted. You're lucky he wasn't waiting here for you."

The building shook harder.

Tatima's shoulders shook under his hands. "It's getting worse."

Jesus. "Some kind of self-destruct thing. I think the building's coming down. I think they're hoping we'll all be stuck inside. We have to move."

Chapter Twenty-one

Journal entry: 10.25.2668 – daytime sometime

We're back in the basement of this old hotel, surrounded by things—creatures, people—I used to loathe and fear. All I can feel is... I don't think I'd say relief, not quite yet. Fairfield is still out there. By the time we made it back to the outer office where I'd left him, he was gone. A trail of blood led down the hall.

I think I've managed to piece together what Fairfield tried to accomplish. I found a newspaper on a desk with a picture of Fairfield and his family. "Fairfield in the Running," it said. His platform? Reuniting the west and east again into a singular United States, like historical times.

Overly ambitious if you ask me, but there you go.

He was the one supplying places like North Woods Outpost with the Ellanol that was killing them. Easy enough, with his position at my Father's company. Grease the right palms in the prison system and the rest is a done deal.

His big push, I guess, was containing the population so the "normal" humans didn't have to feel "threatened" anymore.

Kill my father, take control, wipe out the supes and then claim victory when he brought their population under control. Win, win, and win. His mistress had been a fly in the ointment, I guess—how can you run as a president who's going to keep the supernaturals under control if you're fucking one on the side? So he'd had to kill her, too.

And they call Tatima's kind the parasites? I've been so wrong, and I'm ashamed.

We released everyone we could from their "accommodations" in the lab before the building started to crumble. Some couldn't leave. They were too far gone. I shot a paralyzed shifter stuck in animal form to put it out of its misery—something I never thought would be so hard. I wondered for half a second if it could be saved, but when I tried to pick it up, it whined and protested. I could see the pain in its eyes, and there wasn't any time.

If it were me, I would have wanted death. I'll wonder forever if what I did was right.

As it was, I'm amazed we made it down the stairs before the entire building caved. Some of the creatures have wounds from falling rock and burns from the fire that started up in the stairwells. Fairfield must have set up a plan to destroy the building, should anybody ever catch on to what he was doing. Jesus. He'd have destroyed it with all these creatures locked inside. With us. With Tatima's little boy.

I'm just glad we made it out alive. Whole, is another matter.

***

Ronan looked up when Tatima tapped him on the shoulder. "Hey. How's Valo?"

"I can't get him to wake up, but I'm trying to stay hopeful. I gave him blood, and his wounds have closed. He's alive."

She sat beside him, and Ronan pulled her close. "That's what matters. His body needs to heal, and so does the rest of him. I'm sure the best thing for him is to sleep."

She placed her chin on her fist, nodding. "How are you? You stayed so calm up there."

I wasn't calm. I wanted to tear the walls down with my bear hands.

His heart rate still hadn't calmed. All the fear, the what-ifs. The need to track down Fairfield and finish the job. "I'll be fine." Even as he said the words, his chest ached. So many questions burned holes in his mind that his hair might as well be on fire. One of them had to do with Tatima and where she planned to go once her son was—God willing—stable. Where did they stand, Ronan and her? He still wanted to stay with her, to help offer what protection he could. But he wanted it to be her choice.

"No." She rubbed her hand along his chin. "You aren't. I feel you. This has been so much. A few weeks ago you thought you fought on the same side as Fairfield. I can't imagine such a shift. It must be like the ground under you has disappeared."

Her understanding bound his chest tightly. "That's one way of describing it." He nodded. "I'm hanging in there, though. Fairfield, I can't believe his betrayal. He harmed so many, and then threw them under the bus like they meant nothing." His forehead throbbed at the incomprehensibility of the chain of events that must have led Fairfield to where he'd landed. "I walked into North Woods so pissed. Thinking I'd avenge my father's death. It's hard not to wonder if I could have turned into that kind of a monster."

Cold sweat broke out as he stared at her. She had to have known, but saying it aloud could make her walk away, and he didn't want her to go.

She placed one hand on either side of his face. "You couldn't. You found out what was going on, and you saved me. Someone like him wouldn't have helped me the way you did."

He pressed his face to hers. "It's hard to see now how I could have done anything else."

She smiled. "I can never thank you enough. What you did for me. For all of us..." She looked around. "Everyone here is alive because you helped them escape." She bumped her forehead against his. "We're still hoping to make it over the border." For a moment she was quiet. "I was hoping you'd want to come."

So much for saving the serious talk until later. Regardless, this was what he'd wanted to hear. "I want to." Ronan pulled her to standing and kissed her deeply, smiling when his tongue met one of her fangs. "I hope I can. But, there's something I have to do first."

Chapter Twenty-two

When everybody had been triaged, settled down, and given food—God bless Noah and his shady connections—Ronan prepared to search for Fairfield.

"Are you sure?" Tatima's lips trembled against his ear. "He could be long gone by now."

Ronan drew the night air into his lungs. They stood by the tunnel exit from the hotel, still shrouded in near-dark. He understood her wanting him to stay, but they wouldn't be safe from harm until Ronan got rid of Fairfield.

"No, I'd bet anything he's still close by. He wants that election. He wouldn't disappear yet." Ronan took another breath. "Everybody in this hotel basement is standing in the way of his notoriety." Ronan had rolled this idea over and over in his mind over the past few hours until he had it polished and shiny. Perfect from every angle at which he'd examined Fairfield's perceived brand of insanity, like a weathered stone. The more he turned it over in his head, the more he was certain. "He'll want to be sure we're all dealt with before he disappears. He's got to finish erasing any evidence of his personal and business dealings. He's also injured."

Noah rounded the corner, back from securing the building exterior. "All right, friend, you ready?

Ronan nodded. "I am, thank you." He hugged Tatima tighter in his arms. "Let us do this, so that the rest of you can be safer."

She squeezed her eyes shut, and tears trickled forth. "Please be careful."

"I was kind of thinking I'd go out there naked and hope for the best."

She hardly pretended to laugh. "Stop." She took a step backward.

He squeezed her arms before letting go. "Just take care of Valo."

She had the worst brave face he'd ever seen.

"I just found you. I'm afraid you're going to leave and not come back," she whispered. "The last time we separated almost got you killed. I can hardly breathe."

He kissed her again. "Keep an eye on everyone." He turned to Noah. "I'm ready if you are."

Noah nodded. He turned, taking Tatima's small, pale hands in his. "Let us do this, Tati. I promise I won't let your human get his ass vaporized," he said softly. He grinned at Ronan. "At your service, my friend."

Ronan frowned. He waited until they'd made it to the end of the access tunnel before he asked about the odd exchange. "What the fuck was that? I don't want to make promises to anyone that I'm not sure I can keep."

"Hope has its own power. Sometimes, you have to have some."

Ronan clipped his knife to his belt. "Yeah. You're right. Thanks."

"Where do you intend to look?" Noah's large, dark body blended with the tunnel shadows as they approached street level.

"I started thinking about this tunnel. I remember my father telling me when I was young about a network of underground subway transports this city used in its heyday. It all got bricked over when the economy tanked. Too expensive to maintain." He shivered against the cold and pulled his coat tighter. "I know a length of it passes near where my father's building stood. When I interned there after school, some workers broke through doing maintenance on a gas line. It kept anyone from being able to go to work for days. From what I understand, those tunnels went everywhere."

Noah sniffed at the wind. "Well, if we get close enough, I can catch a scent."

"You're what, part bloodhound?"

Noah chuckled. "For me, detecting pain is sort of a specialty. It's one of the reasons I got into this line of work." He turned to Ronan. "It's not only my own personal grievances, though I do have a few. It's all the others. What was done to the others who were turned, how they were turned, and what came after. I can taste and smell that lingering pain when I get close. World's got far too much."

Ronan pictured Tatima, holding her young child, bleeding and unconscious in her arms. He wanted to be back in that hotel, holding on to them both. Far too much pain was right.

They reached the place his father had shown him, where a station once stood. A cement rectangle showed them the way. "Fuck." Ronan reached for his weapon, hoping he could find a weak spot.

"Stand back," Noah said. "I can do this." The big man reached into his pack and pulled out something like a compact cannon. Nothing as sophisticated as what they'd trained on at North Woods, this thing looked like it had been picked up in one of those underground market swaps. God knew what old cache it had been salvaged from. The outside had a dusty, dark green color, faded lettering, and enough external damage that Ronan wondered if it would even fire until the whoosh and the impact left his ears ringing and his elbows skinned from being knocked backward to the ground.

When Ronan managed to stand again, there was a hole not much bigger around than either of the two men. Under it, an old escalator descended into the tunnel, deteriorating from disuse and covered with rubble.

"Nice," Ronan murmured.

"I do what I can." Noah stood back so Ronan could make his way into the defunct stairwell.

"Where'd you get that thing? Can't be from this century."

"I've met many people in my rescue work. Sometimes they're willing to do favors."

"Seems there's a lot of that among your community."

"Your community now, too."

Ronan tripped over a block of fallen concrete. Of course it was. If they made it back, he wasn't letting Tatima out of arm's reach. "I hadn't realized."

Dust and rock gave way under their feet as they entered the tunnel. They climbed an old turnstile, and Noah pointed with an exaggerated sniff. "This way, I believe."

Down some stairs and alongside a dilapidated track, drops of fresh blood decorated the dirty concrete. Two sets of footprints led away in the dust.

"Well, he's not alone."

Noah nodded and pulled out a high-powered Castiger gun. "As we suspected. So let's stay sharp."

"Nice piece." Ronan nodded at the weapon. The compact laser shot Noah carried cost a ton and wasn't available on the open market. "Another favor?"

"I think maybe you don't completely grasp how much people appreciate getting over that border, my friend." Noah's white-toothed smile lit up the dark.

Ronan smiled back, but went still at the sound of piercing wails in the tunnel. Thunderous pounding beat against the walls, echoing in his ears. Before he could assess what was coming toward them, massive dark shadows were practically on top of them. "What the—"

"Don't tell me the dude's got elementals as his bodyguards. Fucking traitors." Noah fired at a tattooed giant. His shot met with a static bolt of electricity, and sparks flew. "They got the shittiest end of the stick in all that testing business, their bodies react with damn near anything that's got electricity. Something in that mess must still have juice." Noah gestured to the out-of-date track. "Ain't pretty, neither. You'd think they'd want the humans who did that to 'em dead more than anyone."

"So many things make no sense.'" Ronan ducked an errant bolt, thrown by a bald man dressed in boots and leather. "Maybe Fairfield promised them something. Held something over their heads." He fired his weapon, hitting the lightning-throwing thug in the shoulder.

The thug opened his mouth, but a roar of pain came out, wall-shattering in the tunnel.

Ronan pressed his advantage. The elemental conjured another crackle and fizz, and Ronan fired before it launched. The zap went wild anyway, nicking the elemental's shoulder and burning along his back. The elemental tried to push off the concrete of the tunnel, but Ronan gritted his teeth and took a running leap. He landed and they both rolled.

Ronan pulled his knife from his side and plunged it deep into the large male's throat, steeling himself against the strange scream. He thought of the primal screams from North Woods, and wondered if one of these guys was what he'd been hearing.

No scream came, though, only gurgles and blood. He cut across the elemental's throat and was pulling away from a body drained of blood and life when a warm muzzle cozied-up to his temple.

"Where's your pet?"

Ronan stiffened. "She's not my pet."

"Oh, don't play that game. I know what an emotionally bonded parasite looks like. I used to have one."

Ronan tightened his fingers around his knife. That word was making him nauseous. "And you killed her."

"Necessary." Fairfield stooped with pained, jerky movements and growled in his ear. "She went for your father. She had to be put down. She...will be missed."

Ronan risked a glance at Fairfield. "You killed her because she killed my dad." He took a deep breath against the tension in his chest, willing himself to stay calm. "I don't think that's the real reason."

Fairfield scoffed. "I think you know the reason. I'm a married man. A prominent public figure. I have children. I couldn't have a mistress, especially not one of *those*. She had to be taken care of."

A buzz sounded in Ronan's ear. The weapon warming up to fire. "You are fucked-up."

"Fair enough. Now, it seems, you need to be taken care of, too."

Ronan took a risk and lashed back with the knife, sinking the jagged blade deep into Fairfield's ankle. He ducked his head to get clear of the gun, but there was no place to go except into the lifeless chest of the dead guard.

Perhaps it saved him. When Fairfield screamed and tried to shoot anyway, Ronan grabbed the body and pulled it on top of him. The corpse of the bulky elemental did not move easily, but it was enough cover to block Fairfield's errant shot. The old man stumbled, and when he did, Ronan pulled out his own weapon.

He slid from under the blood-slicked body that covered him and stormed over. Fairfield bled from his shoulder and his leg, where Ronan's knife still protruded. Ronan aimed, shaking his head. "You deserve worse for what you did to Tatima."

Fucker had the balls to laugh. "I knew she had claimed you."

"She hasn't claimed me, not really. If she'll have me, then yes. She's mine." He fired once, twice, then a third time, to be completely certain. Tension eased from Ronan's body as red saturated Fairfield's chest.

A shuffle and slide sent Ronan toward the stairs, where he found Noah struggling with another of Fairfield's guards.

A shot from Noah's weapon knocked the giant thug out, but not before Noah sustained damage as well.

Ronan dropped to his knees next to his friend, pressing one hand over a charred wound. "I'm sorry. I should have come alone."

"Then you would have died." Noah's bloody hand gripped his. "You've got a family back there. This was for their good. For all those you rescued. Take care of them." He smiled faintly as he sagged against the dirt-caked wall and let his eyes drift shut.

"Noah. Fuck! No, no, you can't do this. We've got to get all those people to the border. I'm awful with directions." White-hot spikes of adrenaline pushed Ronan's body up under Noah's massive arms. "Come on and get up. Help me out."

"Nah," Noah whispered. "I got cash and weapons stashed in the hotel. You'll be fine."

"Fuck you." Ronan grunted and staggered under the bigger man's bulk. "I'm not leaving you down here." He stopped for a second to listen for the sounds of another attack, but the only noises in the old tunnel were the occasional scrabbling rat or falling rock. Thank fuck.

He needed to find Noah a blood-sucker, if they had any shot at all. After that, he was ready to claim the woman he loved.

Epilogue

After the winters in the northeast, Ronan still couldn't get used to the West Coast. It wasn't a bad thing, but the mild temperatures and the sea spray in their little coastal community always struck him as surreal after the harsh winter they'd endured.

He'd take it.

The trek across the Eastern States had been difficult due to illness and injuries. Some of the rescues didn't survive. Thankfully, they managed with no further fighting. With both candidates in the Eastern States election missing and presumed dead, the government had been busy with bigger concerns than a few stray supernaturals.

Ronan stood from his deck chair to toss a log on the bonfire. Edamom, one of the locals, had brought in crabs to cook right on the beach. Crabs. And corn. How on Earth did this stuff exist here in the Western States when it had been nothing but food shortages in the east? Ronan could only guess that all the unrest in the east had led to more widespread problems.

"Valo!"

The boy, now five, had grown like a weed since they'd settled at the coast. He came running from the other side of the fire. "What, Papa?"

Valo had taken to calling Ronan that, and Ronan found he liked the title. "What do you mean *what*?" He tousled the child's hair. "You said you wanted to be responsible and help your mother, but here you are, dancing around the bonfire."

"Oh. Right."

The boy looked chagrined, but Tatima's hand went to Ronan's shoulder. "He's feeling more independent. I think it's a good sign."

He threaded his fingers with hers. "You're right." He inhaled the scent of the bonfire, taking in the vision of his mate and reminding himself that the warmth meant something good. His nightmares of the things they'd endured at the North Woods Outpost and after still haunted him. He slept with his arms around her so tight he was afraid to let go. "So much has changed."

She smiled. "It has." She nudged him over on the bench where he sat. "Can I join you? I've been helping to clear space for the new arrivals. My feet are tired."

He scooted over and hooked one hand around the curve of her waist, pulling her tightly to his side. "Of course. This memory will keep me company while I'm gone." He kissed her to soothe her look of concern. "It's okay. It'll be a quick trip this time. I promised you no more going over the border."

"I can't help but worry."

He nodded. "One of Noah's kind managed to infiltrate the supermax station in what used to be Missouri. Took the form of a transport manager. All I have to do is help the escapees integrate over on this side, like I've done before."

He never took the ones who were truly dangerous. They had their rules. It was why Noah spent time in the detention centers himself, to evaluate each individual and determine their threat level to society. They had found, however, that most were simply there thanks to people like Fairfield and their desire to "reclaim" society for the "real" humans.

Her arms slid around his. "It may scare me to see you leave, but I'm proud of what you're doing. You've saved so many lives."

"No, that's Noah's doing. I'm just helping those he frees get used to life on the outside again."

She shook her head, her eyes shiny as she stared out at the surf. "Trust me, after living in a box, that's no small thing."

Valo came up then and threw his arms around them, covering them all in wet sand.

Ronan laughed and pretended to push the boy away, then pulled him in with his free arm for a hug. He could not dream of a better life, never mind that what he had now was something he would have once avoided at all costs.

He had a family again. He had love. A purpose. Now, it was everything.

One day, the uprising would be a distant thing in all of their memories, and they would truly find freedom.

Ronan believed this in his heart.

***

THANK YOU for reading In the Arms of the Enemy! I have already been asked if there will be a sequel, and that will depend greatly on reader demand, but I do have an idea for Noah's story that I would LOVE to explore, so please let me know via reviews or by contacting me directly if you would like to read his book! To keep up with *all of my* happenings and future releases, be sure to subscribe to my newsletter[1]. I also love to interact on Twitter[2] and Facebook[3].

ALSO BY ELISABETH STAAB

Contemporary – The Evergreen Grove Series: At the Stars, Acts of Creation, By the Rules

One Week (HaleStorm, Book One)

Nonfiction - Scribbling Women Anthology

Paranormal:

King of Darkness (Chronicles of Yavn, Book One)

Prince of Power (Chronicles of Yavn, Book Two)

Hunter by Night (Chronicles of Yavn, Book Three)

Wild Nights with a Lone Wolf (Lone Wolf, Book One)

Wicked Days with a Lone Wolf (Lone Wolf, Book Two)

Blood Moon Over a Lone Wolf (Lone Wolf, Book Three)

---

1. http://tiny.cc/StaabNews

2. https://twitter.com/ElisabethStaab/

3. https://www.facebook.com/ElisabethStaabRomance/

Acknowledgements

Thank you first and always to my readers, because without you I'm talking to myself in traffic for no reason whatsoever.

Just because a book is shorter doesn't mean it's easier to write. In the Arms of the Enemy is not my longest novel, but it is one that I labored over longer than many others I've written. What started as a quick, fun little dystopian romance grew into "the thing that would not be finished." So with that in mind I have to thank Rhonda Helms, Tere Michaels, and Jena at Practical Proofing, ALL of whom helped me edit the crap out of this book, and who would not let me be lazy and call it "good enough" even when I really wanted to.

HUGE thank you to Amber Belldene for the much-needed gut check, to Melissa Woods and Shelly Small for helping me to give my words a final polish, and to Angela Quarles for being the coolest and most conscientious formatter (and fellow author!) I've had the pleasure of knowing.

Trish Pickyme, your cover art is always gorgeous and so are you. I love you to the moon and back, girl. I'm so thrilled this cover finally got to see the light of day! <3

Thank you always to the Staab Mob, for being awesome. I appreciate your support and your pimpage and your book chatter. Always looking forward to more.

Most of all thank you to the hubs and the kids, without whom this would all be so much harder and infinitely less fulfilling. You guys are my heroes, and you are tattooed on my heart forever.

ABOUT ELISABETH

Elisabeth Staab loves passionate stories and happy endings. Her books have been called "emotionally delicious," "action-packed," and "gloriously snarky." When not writing romance about vampires and werewolves and emotionally wounded boxers (oh, my!), she enjoys date night with her husband, reading with her kids, and marathoning her favorite books or TV series. Keep up with all the latest shenanigans by following her newsletter[4], stopping by ElisabethStaab.com[5], or finding her on Facebook[6] and Twitter[7].

Editing by Rhonda Helms, Tere Michaels, and Practical Proofing

Cover design by Pickyme

This book is a work of fiction. Names, places, and situations are fictitious or are used fictitiously.

---

4.   https://www.myauthorbiz.com/ENewsletter.php?acct=ES1574155922

5.   http://elisabethstaab.com/

6.   https://www.facebook.com/ElisabethStaabRomance

7.   https://twitter.com/ElisabethStaab

Also by Elisabeth Staab

Standalone
Welcome to Evergreen Grove: The Evergreen Grove Box Set
In the Arms of the Enemy

Watch for more at elisabethstaab.com.